Lost *In* Kane

Amanda Smyth lives in bonny Scotland with her own version of Tyler Kane, and loves nothing more than happy ever afters.

She is currently working on book two in the Master series: Forever Kane, and is always happy to hear from new fans.

You can tell her about your happy ever afters at

https://asmythauthor.com

Lost In Kane Master, Book 1 Amanda Smyth

Ebook: Published: 2017 ISBN: 978-1-62210-441-3
Published by Liquid Silver Publishing. Copyright ©
2017, Amanda Smyth.

Print rights: Amanda Smyth 2017 ISBN:
988-0-9956613-3-2

This is a work of fiction. The characters, incidents
and dialogues in this book are of the author's imagi-
nation and are not to be construed as real. Any re-
semblance to actual events or persons, living or dead,
is completely coincidental.

Manufactured in the USA. Email sup-
port@liquidsilverpublishing.com with questions, or
inquiries about Liquid Silver Books, Liquid Silver
Publishing, or Ten West Publishing.

For Mary, for always being there to cheer me on. I will be forever indebted.

With heartfelt thanks to:
Rebecca Gilbert—The best editor in the word, bar none.
Liquid Silver Publishing team, a total dream to work with.
Angie at Angiewatersart.com
for her fantastic cover.
And to you, readers and romantics around the world—
Thank you from the bottom of my heart.

Amanda Smyth

xxx

A Smyth

Lost

In

Kane

Master Novel

#1

TYLER

Glasgow always looked better in the early hours of the morning, the sun just rising, a haze of moisture caressing the air just above the Clyde's deep, dark waters. But this wasn't early morning, and the view from Tyler Kane's office window was doing little to lift his damn mood.

What the fuck had he been thinking? He didn't do the dating shit! Not one night. Not blind. Nothing! Nada. He fucked. Hard! End of conversation.

His little brother owed him big time for this one. Way big!

Scowling hard, Tyler shoved his hands deeper into his pockets. It was only one night. Just one night of being nice and playing the game. After that, he'd drop the girl off, say goodnight, and grab an early evening. Favor to little brother complete. No harm done, and back to sunny Wisconsin at six.

With a snort of frustration, Tyler turned his attention back to the reports on his desk and shrugged off his jacket. He poured himself a much-needed whiskey from the well-stocked cabinet behind his desk, and sat down.

Stuart's voice interrupted his dull mood through the office com.

"Sir?"

"What is it, Stuart?"

"Your gala tickets, sir. Shall I forward them to your Wisconsin or Chicago address?"

"Chicago," he hissed, swirling the whiskey around his mouth with a grimace.

"Yes, sir. I have forwarded the details to your driver and placed a reminder in your diary as per usual."

"Thanks, Stuart."

"You're welcome, sir. Will there be anything else this evening?"

Tyler gulped down the amber liquid, waiting until the burn passed before answering. "Has Daniel gotten back to you with the information I requested on Miss Anna Wright?"

"Nothing yet, sir. Shall I have him fax you the details as soon as he receives them?"

"No. Tell Daniel to phone my mobile as soon as he has something to report."

"Texting him now, sir. Will there be anything else?"

"No. That's it. Go home, Stuart."

"Have a lovely evening, sir."

Yeah, right. Tyler scowled and glanced at his watch—five minutes before eight. He was meeting Frank at nine. He could hit the dungeons, try to work off some of his bad mood with a nine tail. But that would leave him little time for a shower afterwards. Only one thing for it—standing up, he poured himself another whiskey, fingers loosening the tie that had been chafing at his neck all day. Slipping his fingers beneath the knot, he tore the damn thing off and tossed it across his desk. Jeans and T-shirt hung in the adjoining en- suite. Another whiskey and he'd change into them. *Better make that two,* he told himself, and sat old Jack Daniel's down on the desk next to his glass.

*

ANNA

Saturday. The last day in my online virginity auction, and I have no nails left. To say I'm nervous would be the understatement of the century. I'm a nervous frigging wreck. And to top it all off, Steph is expecting me to be sociable and charming to Frank's big brother tonight. How the hell did I get into this mess?

I graze along my nail bed and find nothing left to chew on but jagged little stubs. "You're a fucking idiot, Anna Wright," I mumble to my reflection. A dark-haired girl with large green eyes, paler than yesterday's skin and skinnier than last week's body, looks back dolefully. With a soft sigh, I slide her out of sight and retrieve the only suitable attire I own—a 1920s vintage dress, courtesy of good old Oxfam. Fingering the delicate fabric with love, I lay it across the bed, and begin fishing through my drawers for knickers, suspender belt, and nude stockings. The bra I have chosen is lacey and nude, but even so, the straps will

4

show through the lace of the dress. I glance down at my breasts thoughtfully. They're round and firm with stand-to-attention nipples and no sagging in sight. I cup them in my palms, turn to the left and then to the right. They don't sway or bounce as I move. I might just get away with it. I put the bra back and close the drawer.

Nude dolly shoes fished from under the bed complete the look. Now all I have to do is pin up my hair. The last pin slides into my loose chignon as Steph barges through my door.

"Wow, who pulled out your stopper?" She grins.

"Not too bad yourself," I compliment her. Her sexy Goth look of wedged boots, micro shorts, black vest, and black knee-high socks is a sure winner and will have any male within a fifty-mile radius panting with desire.

And me? Well I'm more of a glance over compared to Steph, and that suits me just fine. Attention isn't something I'm comfortable with.

"So, where we going?" I ask.

"I told Frank we'd meet them in O'Shannigans. A few beers there and then we're off to boogie the night away at the Corinthian." She wiggles her hips dramatically.

5

I wish I were more like her. I shake my head and smile. Maybe tonight I will be.

Forty minutes later, and we're standing in O'Shannigans—local watering hole to under-agers, college grads, and serial gropers. The tables are old wood, scarred with ringed glass stains, and the lamps are Tiffany rip offs. But it's the campus choice, where the drinks are always cheap, and the atmosphere always cheerful.

Sean O'Hare, O'Shannigans' long-standing owner-occupier, slaps his large, hairy hands down before us. His face is ruddy and, as always, he's grinning like a deranged garden gnome.

"What can I get for you, girls?"

"Budweiser and Budweiser please, Sean," yells Stephanie over the din of the band. "And put it on Frank's tab." She juts her chin toward the band. "They're quite good."

Sean nods and rips the top off two Buds.

"Yeah, but a tad too noisy for me. They call themselves 'The Darkness'." He waves his fingers scarily in front of his face, and I can't help but laugh.

"Oh, Anna, you should do that more often, lass. Your face lights up like a fairy lamp when you smile." He moves off down the bar with an infectious grin and a twinkle in his old eyes.

"If he were a few decades younger, he'd be chasing you." Steph chuckles. She takes a long swig from her Bud and sweeps the room with her gaze.

"Yeah, and I'd be running in the opposite direction. Can you see them?" I ask against the lip of my bottle.

"See who?" A familiar male voice filled with humor tickles my right ear.

I shuffle down a stool and Frank Kane—St. Andrew's University rugby hero, and Steph's fiancé—jumps up onto my vacated spot and leans into Steph for a kiss that sets my cheeks aflame.

I look away, embarrassed by their public display of affection and meet *the favor*—aka, Tyler Kane. I've seen photographs of him dotted around Frank's flat on the rare occasions I've been there with Steph. But they in no way prepared me for the real deal, not by a frigging long shot.

My chest constricts. And even though it's rude, I can't help but stare at the man standing before me.

He's dressed in a gray T-shirt, pilot style bomber jacket, and jeans that hug and dip in all the right places. Short dark hair frames his bronzed face with just the right amount of wavy unruliness. And right at this precise millisecond in time, scorching hot dark

7

eyes are scrutinizing me with open amusement. I drop my gaze, cheeks aflame in my embarrassment at having been caught staring.

He eases himself lazily onto the stool next to my own, and my heart rate spikes. *What is wrong with you?* I scream at myself. *You're acting like a horny fucking teenager. Get a grip!*

Reining in the horny hormone I didn't even know I possessed, I lick my lips, wiggle my butt to the left of my seat and slide right off the damn thing to land with a dull thump at Tyler Kane's feet.

Warm fingers instantly glide under my elbow and help me back to vertical.

"Anything broken?" he asks teasingly.

"I'm so sorry. I'm just…really, really, nervous." I slide my arm out from under his grip.

He frowns—not that I blame him—and steps back, allowing me room to dust myself down and reclaim what little dignity I have left.

"You have nothing to apologize for, Miss Wright. How is your bottom?"

"Tender but fine." I divert the conversation away from my butt and back to him. "Stephanie told me you were only here for a few days. Are you here on business, Mr. Kane?"

"Tyler, please." He smiles lazily, and it takes all of my concentration to keep my eyes from straying to his mouth. "And yes, just business. I return home tomorrow."

"America?"

"Wisconsin."

I can't help it, I'm fixated on his lips, the silkiness of them against his strong jaw, his bronzed neck, chest—

Get a grip, Anna, I chastise myself. *Seriously! What the hell is wrong with you tonight?*

He leans forward, his voice rippling seductively across the sensitive skin at the base of my ear. "I do hope you approve of what you see, Anna," he murmurs, sliding a warm hand around my waist and tugging me against six feet two of hard male flesh. This close, he smells exactly how I had expected him to—expensive. I slip out of his grip, reach up, and tuck an escaped strand of hair back behind my ear.

"I wasn't, I mean I was, but not…not like that."

"And by *that*, you mean what exactly, Miss Wright?"

Before I can answer, Frank comes to my rescue by draping an arm around his brother's shoulder and steering the conversation back to good old neutrality.

"Leave her alone, Tyler. She's not *that type* of girl. Steph had to twist her arm to get her to come tonight."

"I'm glad she did," Tyler drawls.

I have never blushed so much in my entire life. And Frank was right—I'm not that type of girl. This guy was pressing buttons I didn't even know I possessed.

"Okay! Enough of this chit-chat. Time's a-wasting!" Steph states and, curling her arm around Frank's waist, she heads for the exit.

Without invitation, Tyler folds his hand around my own and leads me outside.

Ten minutes later, three huge bouncers dressed in formal black—each wearing tiny ear and mouthpieces—eye our passing into Glasgow's most prestigious nightclub with a curt nod of their shaved heads.

Jesus H. Christ. What the hell am I doing? My legs feel like jelly. I don't know this man. In truth, I know nothing of men at all. And yet, here I am, turning into a gelatinous quivering mess of hormones at the mere touch of him.

He narrows his sinfully dark brown eyes quizzically. "You're shivering, Miss Wright. Are you cold?"

I swallow past the lump in my throat and shake my head, my hungry, traitorous eyes lingering on his glorious mouth more than is acceptable or polite.

I wet my lips nervously.

God! How can I want this man to kiss me when I have only just met him? Stupid, stupid, stupid, my inner voice screams at me.

"A little," I lie. There is no way I'm going to let him know that the cold has nothing to do with my shivering. Nothing at all.

A small V forms between his brows. Shit! He knows I'm lying. I tear my gaze from his and look at anything but him.

Letting out that breath he dragged in earlier, he tugs gently at my hand and leads me into what appears—to my untrained eye—to be a private VIP suite.

I glance around at how the other half lives. To my left, there is an overly large corner settee. To my right, a well-stocked bar. And directly before me, an open railing. Four wide steps at its center lead down to a dance floor, which, even from here, I can feel vibrating with movement.

Tyler's hands settle upon my shoulders, and I have to bite down on my lip to keep in the soft mewl of delight jangling for release upon my tongue.

"May I?" he asks.

"Please," I murmur.

He slides the coat free of my shoulders and drapes it across one of the many easy chairs dotted about the

11

room.

I smile and mumble an awkward, "Thank you," not knowing what else to say.

"The pleasure is all mine, Anna."

I squirm under his scrutinizing gaze and slide my hands free of his, grateful that Steph is here to keep me from making a damn fool of myself. I look over my shoulder at her with a plea in my eyes. But Steph only winks and pulls Frank forward toward the dance floor. A lascivious grin spreads across her face. And then she's gone, swallowed up within the jumping, yelling crowd. I let out the breath I have been holding in, walk toward a plump sofa, and sit down.

"Do I make you nervous, Anna?" He sits casually on the sofa's twin.

How does he do that, make his voice so soft, and yet so predatory?

I gulp and nod.

"I'm sorry. That is not my intention. Believe it or not, I'm as disconcerted as you are. Maybe even more so." He frowns.

I fight down a sudden urge to trace my tongue across those frown lines. *Oh, my sweet Lord! What the hell is wrong with me? I'm thinking like a total whore.* I inhale erratically. "I don't do this..." I

12

flounder, looking for the right words and coming up empty.

Grabbing a beer from the table top, Tyler leans forward, his hands draped casually between his knees. "And by *this,* you mean what exactly?" He takes a long drink, eyes fixed on my face over the mouth of his beer bottle.

"Date. I don't—date."

"You have never had a boyfriend?" He sounds incredulous and humorously condescending.

I shake my head, eyes lowered. "No, never." God, this is the strangest conversation I have ever had, bar none.

"May I enquire why?" I don't need to look at him to know he's smiling.

I squirm in my seat. Why the hell are we even talking about this?

"I…" I exhale shakily and pick at the hem of my poor dress. "I have some issues. Dating would complicate those issues." There, that ought to send him running for the hills. *But is that what you want, Anna? Look at him for God's sake. Wouldn't you like to feel those lips on you?*

Would I? Hell, now I'm frowning.

"We all have issues, Anna. It's just a matter of how

13

we choose to deal with them that shapes our lives."

The buzzing of a phone on vibrate fills the air between us. Tyler fishes into his jeans pocket, pulls out his iPhone and checks the screen. "Please excuse me. I have to take this."

I nod, and he's gone, leaving nothing but that deliciously clean, citrusy aroma I'm already beginning to associate with him.

I shouldn't be doing this to myself. In less than a few hours, if everything is agreeable, I will be someone else's to do with as they will. And Tyler Kane will be nothing more than a distant memory.

I swipe a Bud from the table top, swig hard, and push myself vertical. Walking over to the railing that separates me from the busy dance floor, I lean against it.

Paloma Faith is screaming out what she *can't rely on,* and of their own accord, my hips begin to sway.

On the dance floor, Steph is strutting her stuff for all it's worth, and Frank, well, he has eyes and hands only for her. Suddenly, I feel very alone.

"This is a mistake." I shouldn't be here. I'm no good with people and even worse with strangers. Especially when they affect me as much as Mr. Hot does. I'm just begging for trouble to come knocking if I stay.

14

Steph spots me above the heads of the dancers and waves me down. I shake my head and point to my bottle. A slight breeze against my back and I know that Tyler has walked back into the room.

I hold my breath and concentrate all my energy on not turning around.

"Do you dance, Miss Wright?" His voice is a dark purr of seduction and my heart flips in reply. I do dance. It's the only thing I do that I don't have to think about doing, and I do it well. But not tonight, and most definitely not with this man.

He stands millimeters from my side on the platform, leaning against the railing, his back to the dancers as he gazes at me with that damned amused expression in his eyes again.

I hold his gaze. I am not a gazelle, and he is not a damned lion. I should not be afraid of this man—or how he makes me feel. The words spill out before I can stop them. "I dance well, Mr. Kane. And you? Do you dance?"

His grin widens but he shakes his head. "Unfortunately, no. I'm more of an outdoor man. Motorcycle racing, rock climbing, that sort of thing."

I nod. It makes perfect sense. Tyler Kane's body is toned, tanned and lithe. And a body like that doesn't come without hard work and a whole lot of vigorous activity. My eyes drift involuntarily to his chest and the muscles bunched under his gray T-shirt. Damn him for being so good-looking! Dragging my eyes from his chest, I flick through my frazzled brain for something safe to say. "So, you're Frank's big brother?" *That's the best you can do, Anna? Fucking Hell!*

"Half-brother. We share the same birth mother, a love of sports, and an uncanny ability to make complete asses of ourselves on the dance floor." He flicks his eyes toward his brother, who is thumping about like Shrek and grinning like he owns the floor—which, in a way, I guess he does because, right now, other dancers are jumping out of his way with Usain Bolt speed.

I laugh heartily and without reservation at the spectacle that is Frank Kane on the dance floor.

"You have a beautiful laugh, Anna. It's uncensored and free. Quite rare in the circles I travel."

I stop laughing and look at him. Really look.

He clears his throat and inches closer, nodding his head toward his brother. "What about you? Any embarrassing family members lurking about?"

I shake my head firmly. "No. No family lurking anywhere."

16

"I envy you that freedom, Miss Wright. Family can be a hindrance in finding one's identity in the world."

I lock eyes with his. How can he say that? He has no idea! None at all.

"You have no idea what you are talking about, Mr. Kane. My life…is by no means enviable, I assure you."

He studies me for a moment, a scowl marring his perfect features. And for a second, he looks almost vulnerable. Then he smiles—a forced smile that tells of a man who has mastered the art of keeping his secrets secret—and points to my drink.

"Your beer is almost finished, Anna. Can I get you something else? Maybe something more befitting your attire?"

"Yes. Thank you." I flip my gaze away from the tidal wave of movement on the dance floor and reseat myself on the easy chair I vacated only minutes earlier, thankful the conversation has moved on to safer ground. "Do you think they'll leave the dance floor sometime tonight?"

He hands me a delicate flute of fizzing wine and sits down beside me on the arm of my chair.

I look at him, really look at him, this man who disturbs my equilibrium so badly, and I find him brimming with everything and lacking in nothing. I sip at

17

the wine and draw back in surprise that I'm, actually enjoying it. "Mmmm. This is nice. Most of the wines I've tried taste like vinegar."

"Then you have never tasted wine."

I flush under his stare and take a larger sip.

He watches me without apology.

The experience of having those dark eyes focused solely on me is unnerving. "I'm sorry. But can you not do that?"

"Do what?"

He raises an eyebrow and something coils warmly within my stomach.

Is he playing with me? The thought adds fire to my words. "I don't like being stared at, Mr. Kane."

"I wasn't staring, Miss Wright. I was admiring a beautiful woman, as is the right of any red-blooded male. Would you rather I ignore you, and we play the game of feigned disinterest? Because I don't think I can do that. You intrigue me too much."

"I'm just another rotten class statistic, Mr. Kane. People like you and me—we shouldn't even be in the same room."

He cocks that damn eyebrow again, and I melt. Sweet Lord, why does he have to be so fucking hot? I drain my glass dry in one quick gulp.

"Is that really how you think of yourself, Miss Wright?"

"It's what I am, Mr. Kane." I pull myself up from my chair, set the wine glass down and lift my coat from the chair he draped it across earlier. "Excuse me, but it's obvious we have nothing in common. Enjoy the rest of your evening, Mr. Kane."

"I don't—" he jumps up and gently but firmly takes my coat from my hands, "pretend to know what inferiority chip that outburst came from. But I have no intention of excusing you. You're going to sit back down in that damn chair and listen to what I have to say to you. Now be the good girl I hope you are and sit."

Anger bubbles into my veins. Anger at Steph for putting me in this position in the first place. Anger at myself for wilting like a lustful slut in front of a man I know absolutely nothing about. And anger at him for drawing out my insecurities and calling me on them.

Biting my lip against the obscenities rising there, I place my hand on the door handle and yank down hard.

Tyler is on me in an instant, his hand slamming the door back on itself, his body immobilizing my own with its warm weight.

19

"I said sit. Or do I have to make you?" His eyes glitter menacingly.

"You wouldn't dare."

"Try me," he growls.

I wriggle against him, trying to free myself from his oppressive weight. The action only succeeds in forcing a curse from his lips, and gripping my chin, Tyler tilts my face up to meet his.

For what seems an eternity, but can be no more than mere seconds, he holds my gaze. Then, with a heavy sigh, he steps back and points one finger toward a chair.

I scamper toward it and sit, eyes wide, hands clenched, and a traitorous heart hammering within my chest.

Tyler grabs a bar stool, plonks it down before me, and straddles it casually.

"That phone call I just took was about you, Miss Wright. Twenty-two years of you, to be precise.

"You ran a check on me?"

He nods.

"How fucking, dare you."

"I dare, Miss Wright, because I can. You should be honored. I don't usually go to these lengths to get laid, but for you, I'm more than willing to make an exception. Like I said earlier, you intrigue me—more so after what I have just been informed of."

"Shit." *He knows about the auction!* "You know about the auction," I whisper.

He nods slowly, dark eyes scrutinizing me.

I wilt under that gaze, open my mouth to speak, and come up empty.

"It ended three minutes ago. Aren't you curious to know what the winning bid was, Anna?"

I can do nothing but look into his eyes—frozen like prey in front of a hunter.

He loses the chair and sits down next to me, his body leaning so far into mine that any personal space is gone. Soft, warm fingers trail a line of fire across my neck. I close my eyes, breath quickening with every soft stroke of his skin against my own.

"I just paid a small fortune for your virtue, little Anna. And all because I don't want anyone else to have what I craved the first instant I saw you. The fact that you're a virgin..." He smiles wickedly and, using his weight, forces me horizontal across the settee. Acting on nothing more than primal instinct, my thighs part, allowing him to nestle firmly in the space provided.

I gasp at the intensity of his desire pulsating against

my sex and shut my eyes against the barrage of emotions raging through my veins.

"Open your eyes, Anna. Look at me."

Biting hard into the plump flesh of my bottom lip, I do as I am told, and open my eyes.

"For the next four weeks, I own you, Anna Wright. You must do as I say. Is that not correct?"

"No," I state with more bravado than I feel. "Both parties must agree to the terms before an agreement can be reached. And the auction was for one—" My voice catches on a high note as his fingers slide seductively up my inner thigh. "One week. Not four...". *Oh sweet Jesus, how am I not combusting already?*

A tortured groan rumbles from somewhere deep in his chest and he closes his eyes, his fingers stilled on the notch of my garter fastening. He curses something unintelligible and pulls back, eyes wild "Fuck, you really know how to play with fire, Miss Wright. Stockings for fuck's sake."

I blink in stunned mode, not knowing what to do with the emotions that are coursing through me like wildfire. "I...I always wear them. They make me feel good."

"Yeah, you and me both, baby. For one so innocent, you sure as hell know how to torture a man, Miss

Wright. Jesus!"

"I don't understand." I honestly don't. I am bewildered by this man falling apart before me.

He glowers at me and sits down hard, repositioning the large bulge in his jeans as he speaks. "Okay. So…" He rakes his fingers irritably through his hair. "Terms as you stated in your advertisement. Obviously, I like what I see and hear. Do you have any reservations about my appearance, Anna?"

I sit up, smooth down my dress, and retrieving a pre-filled glass from the table, drain it in one gulp.

"Anna, do you like what you see?" he demands.

I nod without looking at him. "Yes."

He settles back into his chair, his gaze predatory. "Show me."

"I'm sorry?"

"Show me."

Bastard. He's trying to cow me. *Wrong fucking move, buddy. I have spent my life backing down, but not tonight, and certainly not to Tyler Kane.*

Wiping hands slick with sweat across my knees, I stand up, and leaning low, I graze my lips across his, hoping to God I don't look as idiotic as I feel.

His lips remain closed.

Not to be beaten, and acting on nothing but good

23

old primal instinct, I drift my hand across his erection.

His hand instantly snaps onto my wrist. "Much as I would like to show and tell, baby, we have some fine points to iron out before tomorrow."

"Tomorrow?"

"The auction has ended, Anna. I won. The money in question has been transferred into your named bank account. We have had our first meeting. I want you, and I know that you want me. So tomorrow you will travel with me to my home in Wisconsin, and I will take what I paid for."

I should be running hell for leather away from this man. Gods above, I know I should, but something tells me Tyler Kane isn't the type of person you run from unless you can run faster than he can. I know I can't, and truth be told, why would I want to? Tyler Kane is one hot-looking guy, and I won't ever have to worry about money again. I can complete my degree without fear of, well…anything. But there's something niggling at me; a question I need answered before we go any further.

"Why did you bid for me, Mr. Kane? I mean it's obvious you don't have to pay to get laid. So why start now?"

"Because you have what I want without the baggage of a relationship," he states.

"So, you what? You go around paying obscene amounts of money so that you can fuck virgins?" I don't try to hide the contempt in my voice.

He shakes his head. "You make it sound dirty, Miss Wright. And just for the record, I have never had the pleasure of *'fucking a virgin'* before. You will be my first and my last. I try not to repeat experiences if I can help it."

I roll my shoulders, straighten my back, and nod my head. "And if I have certain conditions, Mr. Kane?"

His eyes zoom in on my mouth, and a strange pulsating begins deep in my groin. I squirm in my seat and cross suddenly trembling legs.

He smiles as if he knows something I don't. "I would be disappointed if you didn't, Miss Wright. What are your conditions?"

I inhale, hold, and close my eyes.

"No filming or pictures, no third parties and..." a small tremor runs through me, "the thought of being intimate with anyone, even you, terrifies the hell out of me."

"Only because you do not understand your sensuality yet, Anna. I will teach you. Which brings me to my

25

next point." He fists his palms and flares his nostrils as if he too is fighting some inner conflict. "You will give me four weeks of your time. Not one as stated in your advert. During that time, you will do as I say, when I say, without argument. You will wear what I buy for you, and you will submit to me completely and without hesitation wherever, and whenever."

I gulp, eyes wide. I can't argue the four weeks. Tyler probably knows I have five weeks before the new term begins anyway. He seems to know just about everything else about me. I nod mutely.

"Good. We leave tomorrow at six. You have a valid passport I take it?"

I am vaguely grateful that I have a passport. Due wholly to Steph, who paid for me to get one. *Just in case,* she had said. I never thought I would ever get to use it. "Yes, I have a passport."

"Then my driver will pick you up at five. You needn't bring anything other than your delectable self. I will take you shopping for a more *suitable* wardrobe when we get there. And training will start as soon as my doctor confirms your virginity and health status. In the intervening period, you will spend your time learning the basics of what I will require from you." He smiles lopsidedly, and I forget all about my dislike of this man and his domineering nature.

"Training?" *What the hell is this man planning to do to me?* I lick suddenly dry lips, and a small muscle twitches in his jaw.

"Yes, training. I intend to show you what that delicious looking tongue of yours was made for, Miss Wright."

Oh, my God. I twist uncomfortably in my seat as his words stoke the raging fire within me.

Suddenly, Steph's head appears above the bannister with Frank stuck behind her like a second limb. She looks from Tyler to me and frowns, no doubt taking in my ruffled appearance and ashen look.

"You okay, Anna?"

Mr. Hot stands and retrieves our jackets.

"Anna was just saying she feels queasy. I offered to escort her home."

Oh shit!

"Anna?" Steph asks, ears pricked and hackles up.

I reassure her with a smile. "I just need to get away from this heat. Some fresh air, and I'll be as right as rain again."

Steph's blue eyes narrow in on Tyler. "Well, I'll be popping in on you when I get back."

I almost laugh. Steph's letting Tyler know that he better not be there when she gets back. I bite my tongue and nod vigorously. "I'll probably be in bed. So just latch the door again on your way out. Catch you later, Frank."

"Night, Anna. Ty, bro. Behave."

Tyler nods, opens the door, and ushers me out of the club, his hand warm and firm against the small of my back.

ANNA

There is a vibrancy to Glasgow City that exists nowhere else in Scotland.

It's a vibrancy that—as Tyler Kane's skin touches my own—I feel now. One that has nothing to do with Glasgow, and a lot to do with this man who guides me through milling smokers, and laughing pedestrians, to an empty space of pavement where he slides me back into my coat. "You hungry, Anna?"

I flush red and squirm beneath that heated gaze. He chuckles and shakes his head.

"I'm talking about sustenance, Miss Wright." His dark eyes flash with juvenile humor. "Although if you keep squirming like that, I might be tempted to take you right here and now, and to hell with the details."

Oh, jings.

I'm so caught up in him that I don't see the group of revelers until it is too late, and I'm being body bumped without apology, into Tyler Kane's hard, warm body. Strong arms tighten protectively around me.

I sag into those arms and let my head fall to where his heart thumps loudest. For a moment, there is nothing but the solid beat of that heart, and then he tilts my face up to meet his gaze. His lips are pinched tight, his brows drawn. He looks like a man struggling against something he doesn't understand, and losing.

I bite my tongue between my teeth, unable to peel myself from the contact.

Tyler's hands tighten around me, and with a low growl, he walks me backwards into the alley that runs the length of the club, his weight pinioning me against the rough, graffiti-covered wall. My heart hammers within my chest, and with horror, I realize I'm seriously turned on. This is too much too fast—twenty-two years of nothing and then...Sweet Lord, I am so done for.

Full lips hover over my own, and I tense as long skillful fingers gently circle my throat, holding me immobile as warm lips trace a line of fire down my throat toward my chest. Hooking the fingers of his free hand under the straps of my dress, he slides the flimsy material down. It pools around my waist with a soft whisper of air. I shiver, my breath quickening as

30

he dips his head and suckles a nipple until it elongates and stiffens beneath his expert tongue. I lose myself to the sheer delight of it all and close my eyes on a gasp of undiluted pleasure.

And then it's over. I open my eyes. Tyler is re-covering me, his breathing as erratic as my own, his fingers trembling but sure in their task.

Angrier than I have ever felt, I push him back, pull my coat around me and march as far as I can away from him. Embarrassed doesn't even begin to cover how I feel right now.

How could you? I berate myself. *He doesn't have to buy your cherry, baby. You're literally throwing it at him, for fuck's sake!*

Tyler grabs my elbow and spins me around to face him. Tears flood my eyes.

"I feel like a damned science experiment. Why? Why did you just do that?"

He yanks me hard against him yet again and, grabbing my wrist, forces my hand down to his groin.

I gasp and try to pull back, but Tyler only locks my wrist in a vice-like grip that allows no movement other than what he permits. His erection strains between us, pulsing against my palm like a caged animal. My eyes widen. I have read of this, fantasized about what it would feel like, but this—*Sweet Jesus! It's fucking huge!*

"How does that fit...in me?" I croak.

He loosens his grip, his breathing labored and harsh.

"I look forward to showing you, baby, but for now, I want you to *feel* what you do to me. If I hadn't let you go back there, I wouldn't have been able to stop. I don't want your first time to be against the back wall of a nightclub in an alley. Anna—" He tucks a stray strand of hair back into place behind my ear. "I want this deal to benefit us both. Do you understand?"

"I think so."

"Good girl." He smiles and kisses my nose. "I think we should go before you destroy my good intentions, Miss Wright. I believe we had been talking about food before you ruined my noble intentions to behave. Yes?"

I nod, still breathless.

"Food it is then." He extends his hand out to me, and after a moment's hesitation, I take it.

We walk in comfortable silence for several minutes before Tyler breaks the peace. "What's going on behind those lovely eyes of yours, Anna?"

I shrug. "I was remembering what you said back

there in the club."

He cocks an eyebrow and waits for me to finish the sentence, curiosity written clear as day all over his chiseled face.

"You're going to have to be more specific, Anna. I said a lot of things back in that club."

"The bit about you not dating."

"I don't. Is that a problem?"

"Not a problem, no. Just strange."

A few balconette bras and micro denims stroll past and eye him suggestively. Tyler doesn't even acknowledge their scantily clad existence, or any of the others we pass as we walk, and on a Saturday night on Buchanan Street, there are many.

"And you are an expert on what's normal and what's not, Anna?"

"I never said I was."

"But you consider it abnormal that I do not waste my time with a social ritual that, ninety-nine percent of the time, will lead to sex anyway? Let me put it another way. How many dates have you been on?"

I squirm under his amused gaze.

"How many, Anna?"

"Two, three maybe."

"In the past week?"

I bite my lip and shake my head, feeling every inch the novice I am.

"Jesus, Anna." His tone is one of astonishment. "How the hell has someone like you stayed under the radar for so goddamn long?"

"Someone like me?"

"Sexy, innocent, beautiful, intelligent. You want me to go on?"

"I don't think of myself like that, Mr. Kane. And the dates I went on were under protest."

"Let me guess. Steph?" He chuckles and my heart skips at the sweet, sweet sound.

I nod.

"And the men she set you up with?"

"Like I said before, Mr. Kane, I'm not the dating type. Some people get the message quicker than others do."

"Ahhh, but we're not on a date, Anna. I am simply inspecting my newest purchase."

"You really are a twisted bastard, aren't you?" The words are out before I can stop them.

But instead of taking offence, Tyler nods, his dark eyes alight with humor. "Oh, baby, I cannot wait to show you just how twisted I can be. Ladies first."

With his splayed hand on my lower back, Tyler

opens one of two glass doors stenciled with the restaurant's name, and guides me inside.

A well-spoken, well-groomed man greets us and leads us to the only available table within the room. I smile my thanks as he seats me, and with an answering smile, he steps back into the hive of activity that surrounds us.

I look at Tyler. He's examining the menu. I open my own menu. Tyler shakes his head. "One thing you should know about me, Anna. I like my women subservient. Put the menu back where you found it."

"And if I say no?"

Tyler sets down his menu. He smiles, his dark gaze settled on my mouth in a hunter-to-prey intensity that coils the muscles in my stomach.

"Then I will clear this table and fuck you right here, right now in full view of everyone around us."

Jesus. "You wouldn't dare." *Would he?*

"Doggy style. Right here. Right now."

Something tells me he would do just that. Gulping, I place the menu back on the table.

"Good girl." He signals the waiter back over and orders "two shrimp Fra Diavolo and a bottle of Krug Clos." I have no idea what he just said. The only wines I can pronounce are single syllable ones. Five if you count Pinot Grigio.

The waiter shifts nervously on his feet. "That particular brand is eight hundred pounds a bottle, sir."

Tyler stares at the waiter, his eyes flinty. "Just bring me the damn bottle," he growls, pushing the menus back into the waiter's chest and discarding him with a flick of his hand and a look capable of freezing flame.

The waiter turns tail and flees.

"You didn't have to be so rude. The poor man was only doing his job."

"I'll leave a generous tip for his services,"

I grimace. "That's not what I meant. You can't erase a wrong done with cash."

He smiles, but it doesn't reach his eyes. "You think I should apologize, Anna?"

"You really need me to answer that? Seriously?"

"And if I refuse?"

"You won't."

"I won't?" He cocks an eyebrow.

"No." I shake my head. "You won't, because even you aren't that big a dick." I hold his stare, green eyes on brown and after what seems an eternity, Tyler chuckles.

"I can't believe you just called me a dick."

"Would you prefer I called you something else?"

He snorts out a full-bodied laugh that draws the attention of every warm-blooded woman in the restaurant, maybe even a few men too.

"Oh, honey, you have no idea. But back to the subject of my rudeness, I will of course, apologize.

Truce?"

I nod and he smiles, his eyes glittering with returned good humor. The waiter approaches, uncorks the wine, pours, and waits. Tyler nods his approval and our glasses are filled before our attendant again removes himself from our vicinity.

I stare at Tyler and with a muttered curse, he unfolds himself from a chair that seems too small for his muscular frame and walks over to the poor man he had barked at only minutes before.

I watch curiously, wondering how the hell I am going to survive four weeks with this volatile man. He is arrogant, cold, hot, scary and everything else between. In short, he's an emotional conundrum.

He finishes his conversation with the offended waiter with an apologetic smile and walks back to me with every female eye in the restaurant trained on his passing, including mine. I can't help it. Tyler Kane's appearance screams long hours of pleasure and virility. Shit, just looking at him turns me on.

He holds my gaze as he sits, long legs stretching out beneath the table to rest against my own.

"I would not have done that for anyone else, Anna. You should feel privileged."

"No, I feel sad that you had to be coerced into treating another human being with respect."

He cocks his head to the side, and I mirror his action. He sips his wine, I sip mine, and our eyes lock. He licks the rim of the glass, and I cave in and look away. He chuckles darkly.

A delicate cough diverts my attention, and a plate of food is placed before me. I look at the plate's contents and sniff tentatively.

"Devil's shrimp," Tyler provides in answer to my look of alarm.

He skewers a shrimp and pops it into his mouth.

I lower my fork and lift my glass.

"Is there something wrong with the food, Anna?"

"Other than the fact that I didn't order it?"

He bites down whatever he was about to say and drains his glass.

I summon the waiter over, order chocolate fudge cake with cream, and offer a shy smile and a soft "thank you."

The waiter smiles back and removes the offending

plate. Seconds later, and he has returned with my choice of vegetarian-friendly dessert from the dessert cart. He proceeds to make a fuss over arranging it and pouring the cream. I thank him and he leaves, only to hover nearby.

"For God's sake. Do all men fawn over you like that?"

I smile and shrug, my mouth full of delicious chocolate cake and fluffy sweet cream.

Tyler mutters harshly under his breath and pushes his half-eaten meal away with attitude.

I smile inwardly. Round one to me. *Go, Anna,* my inner voice yells in triumph.

Twenty-five minutes later, and we are outside on the pavement again.

He hasn't said one word to me since the overly helpful waiter event. Sighing, I walk on ahead of him. A firm hand manacles my wrist and pulls me back. "My driver is on the way. I'll drop you off at your flat."

"I want to walk. It's not that far from here, and frankly, I could do with the fresh air. I'll see you tomorrow morning."

A shiny black BMW rolls to a stop in front of us and draws admiring looks from passing motorists and pedestrians alike. The driver's door opens and an older man exits the vehicle. Without a word, he opens the passenger door and stands sentry at its side.

Tyler shakes his head. "Change of plans, Mark. Drive ahead to 45 Greenling Avenue, please. The lady wants to walk."

Mark nods and reseats himself behind the driver's wheel.

I gawp at the man before me. "How did you know my address?"

"I told you in the club. I ran a check on you."

"You can't...Argh!" I scream, "You just can't do things like that! It's called invasion of privacy or some damn thing along those lines."

"No. It's called doing my homework. I wanted to know about you. You probably wouldn't have told me anything worth knowing so..." He runs his hand across the back of his neck and scowls. "I don't understand why you're so offended. I saved you from some online pervert from God knows where."

I sigh in exasperation. "I can't do this. I'm sorry, but the deal's off. Excuse me." I shoulder past him only to be grabbed back. I pull against his grip.

"The more you try to escape me, Anna, the more it will hurt."

I narrow my eyes, yank hard, and am rewarded with

bone-crushing pain. Tears moisten my eyes and spill across my cheeks.

"You're hurting me," I whisper.

He pulls me in closer, his face mere inches from my own. "Then stop fighting me," he hisses.

"I didn't know I was," I murmur sadly.

He lets go, looking like a man who has just been slapped and doesn't know how to react.

I stumble back but don't run. He is a controlling son of a bitch with serious overbearing issues, but he is also right in everything he has said. This is all on me. My issues have gotten me here, not his. I agreed to sell my virtue and my time and—truth be told—the way he looks, the way he affects me, I would have been putty in his hands after just one date. I shouldn't be making this his issue. With a resigned sigh, I weave my fingers through his.

"You said the deal was off?" he mumbles with a frown.

I shake my head, trying not to think how good his fingers feel against my own and failing miserably.

"Truth be told, you're better looking than an old pervert, and I need the money."

"May I enquire as to why you need the money so badly?"

41

I inhale and hold. How do I answer? I watch Tyler Kane looking at me and shock myself by wanting to tell him. *Jesus!* I exhale in a *don't think about it, just do it* rush and—

"There are people in my life, Mr. Kane, people I owe an enormous debt of gratitude to. The money will go a small way in repaying some of that debt and getting me to where they believe I should be."

"And that place is where, Miss Wright?"

"Anywhere but in a sleeping bag under a bridge in the middle of winter, Mr. Kane."

A small muscle begins to twitch along his jaw line, but other than that, Tyler Kane is motionless. "You slept on the streets, Miss Wright?"

"I *lived* on the streets, Mr. Kane, and I would still be there now if it weren't for those people."

He stops, and for a few minutes, we simply stare at each other.

"It seems you are home, Miss Wright."

Those weren't the words I was expecting. Disappointment floods through me. I slide my hand from beneath his and nod, not trusting what might come out of my mouth if I speak. I climb the steps to my little flat without looking back.

"Miss Wright!"

I stop and turn, one foot in, one foot out.

"My driver will be here to collect you at five a.m. You will need only your passport."

I nod, smile, close the door on tomorrow, Tyler Kane, and all the complications he brings with him.

TYLER

His cock twitched and thickened the moment he set eyes on her, and hours later it was still twitching, wetting his thigh with milky moisture, and tightening his balls painfully.

Tyler scowled and kicked a stone ahead into a dirty litter-strewn puddle. This wasn't how his night was supposed to have gone, but then he hadn't expected to meet the delectable Miss Wright. He hadn't been lying when he said she intrigued him. Anna Wright was the opposite of everything he liked in his women—shy, delicate, fumbling, innocent to the point of stupidity. But damn, he wanted her! Just being in her company—Tyler growled and slapped down the desire to turn back around and knock on her door. *Keep walking, Ty. You're a fucking Master. Behave like it!*

His car pulled to a stop several feet in front of him, and seconds later, Tyler was sliding himself into the back seat, privacy window between himself and his driver all the way up. His cock throbbed heavily against his thigh but he ignored it. Self-denial was all part of the game. A game he would take pleasure teaching Miss Wright the rules of. His lips widened into a grin. He had never had a virgin before, and the thought of Anna Wright spread and shackled over his whipping bench, her tight little...His balls jerked and his cock exploded, violently soaking his jeans in an orgasm that just kept on rolling. "Ahhh. Fuck."

When his cock had again deflated to manageable proportions, he took off his jacket and tied it around his waist, the arms only just hiding his loss of control. He was a Dom for fuck's sake. This should *not* be happening to him!

"We're here, sir."

With a scowl of self-disgust, Tyler exited the car and entered the waiting elevator.

"Will you be needing the car again tonight, sir?"

Tyler shook his head, and taking the plastic key card from his back pocket, he scanned it across the glass insert in the metal wall. "Good night, Mark."

The doors sluiced shut and he sagged wearily back against the wall as the lift propelled him upwards toward his apartment.

He had never met anyone quite like Anna Wright

before, and he didn't know whether to run or stand his ground. Something told him it was too late for running. Even if he boarded his flight tomorrow without Anna Wright at his side, he knew it would only be a matter of time before he came back to claim her. Maybe fucking the girl would end this nonsense once and for all. His cock hardened again just at the mere thought of it, while his phone buzzed to life against his thigh. Tyler fished it from his pocket quickly. Maybe it was her.

Disappointment flooded through him when he remembered he hadn't given her his cell number. He would rectify that mistake in the morning.

The elevator doors pinged open, and he stepped out into his apartment, throwing the vibrating phone from him and heading straight toward the bathroom. Maybe a cold shower would dampen his desire? It was worth a try. Anything was worth a try if it erased Anna fucking Wright from his mind. Even if only for a few minutes.

*

ANNA

I wake up to banging and a head that feels like it's been tenderized with a meat mallet.

"Shit." I roll onto my side and squint at my watch. 04:25 blinks back at me in neon green numerals.

Groaning, I pull the covers up and over my head. Who the hell would be insane enough to get up at this time?

You know who. American, abs like a rock, hung like a fu—

"Okay! I get it." I hiss and kick off my cozy duvet with a scowl.

The banging begins again, causing my front door to vibrate in protest. "Jesus. Hold your horses, I'm coming. Just…Owww! Shit!" I rub at the suddenly disabled toe and hop my way toward the offensive banging. Still rubbing my foot, I fumble the door open.

"Why aren't you dressed?" He strides past me, all six

47

feet two of annoying perfection and glowering annoyance.

"Probably because it's still night time. You know—time for *sleep*."

"I don't have time for this, Anna. Get dressed." He strides past me. "Where's your passport?"

"What?"

"Your passport!"

"In the kitchen, on the work top!" I push past him, grab the passport, and push it into his chest.

He may be Viagra on legs, but at this time in the morning, I really couldn't care less.

"I need a coffee. You want one?"

"I'll make it. Go shower and dress. We don't have much time."

"*We don't have much time,*" I mimic and head off to the bathroom leaving an irritated Tyler Kane behind.

Some people greet the dawn with fifty press-ups and a smile to rival the sun. They're fricking nutters. There are also those who look good at five in the damned morning. I'm not one of them. In fact, as I look at my god-awful reflection in the mirror, I would go so far as to say that a naked lab rat looks better and healthier than I do right now. I push the mirror away and nimbly twist my hair into a simple side braid.

"Coffee's ready whenever you are!"

I ignore him— as much as anyone can ignore, Tyler Kane—and squeeze myself into black skinny jeans and a black sweater that thankfully, I remembered to lay out in advance last night. I zip up, smooth down, and finish off the look with a spray of Anais Anais and black and white knock-off Vans.

Good to go. *Well, as good as I'm going to get.* I yank open the door, and pull my coffee mug free of Tyler Kane's long smooth fingers.

"You said five." I take a tentative sip. Damn! It's good. I drink it down without reservation.

He examines his Rolex—*of course, what else!*—with a puckered brow. "It is five."

"Now it is." I roll my eyes, grab my old Samsung from the kitchen counter, and drain what remains of my coffee noisily.

Tyler relieves me of my mug and bangs it down on the radiator cover beside the door.

"I wasn't finished with that." Who the hell does this guy think he is?

"You are now."

"You always push people about like this, Mr. Kane? Or is it just me?"

"If you hadn't placed that ad I wouldn't be here to

push you about. Where're your keys?"

I shut up. Tyler's right. It is all my fault. My fault for being poor. My fault for selling the only thing I had left to sell to a stunningly beautiful but bullish male with serious domineering tendencies. All my fucking fault!

"Keys," he repeats, palm open.

"On the hook in front of you," I snipe.

He grabs the keys from the hook and proceeds to lock up quicker than I ever have, or ever will.

Two minutes later, and I am sinking into dark leather. Tyler sits beside me, his hand settling across my thigh in full possessive mode.

As usual, my heart jumps. I need a distraction, anything to keep my mind off how good his hand feels. I look out the window and see nothing worth seeing—a gray ominous-looking sky, nearby empty roads and a few early morning joggers who have nothing to prove except how boring their lives really are.

A few dots of rain plop against the glass, then a few more, until suddenly, the whole window looks like a water-battered shower screen.

Beside me, Tyler has snapped open his phone and is barking into it in a language that sounds like Daffy Duck on drugs.

I turn my attention back to the rain. When I was younger, days like this would have been an adventure waiting to happen. Now they just make me sad with longing for…I don't know what.

"Where are you, Anna?"

I turn my head and stare vacantly into his eyes, still lost in my moment of melancholy.

"I'm nowhere," I answer truthfully.

Tyler takes my hand and folds it within his own. His fingers feel robust and safe, all traces of his earlier obnoxious self, gone.

I like him better this way.

"I haven't been there before." He smirks. "What's the weather like?"

"Raining." I grin shyly and tilt my head, looking at him for the first time since he picked me up. He's more formal than he was yesterday, wearing tailored black slacks, shirt and thirties-style waistcoat. The look suits him, but then I doubt if anything wouldn't suit him.

"How many languages do you speak?" I ask curiously.

"Five. You?"

"I always wanted to learn Italian."

"Why didn't you?"

"Oh, I don't know, maybe something to do with the fact that I scraped an existence on the streets."

"I'm sorry, Anna. When I look at you, I forget the hardships you must have endured."

"You're not looking closely enough then. My scars are there for all to see, Mr. Kane. You just choose not to see them," I murmur and turn back to the road.

"Anna…" He swivels in his seat and gently turns my face around to meet his. "Last night, I met a young woman lost in the wrong time frame. She left me breathless, and she left me confused. That has never happened to me before. And I need to know why it happened at all."

He tips his head to the side, dark eyes on my lips. I know he's going to kiss me. Hell, I want him to, who wouldn't? But I can't. Physically and mentally, I'm already hunched on the running block just waiting for that damn gun to explode, and Tyler Kane is my fucking trigger.

His lips move in, such gloriously full lips. I whimper, close my eyes, and ball my fists until my palms sting with nail bite.

I sense him pause, his breath kissing my face so softly, I want to weep at my inability to respond.

"Anna. Look at me."

I shake my head and taste blood on my teeth from biting down too hard on my tongue.

He inhales sharply, and so quickly I don't know it's happening, he strokes my bottom lip with the silky smoothness of his thumb.

I groan into his touch, every fiber of me quivering with need, and fear, and all the things that exist between.

"I will not hurt you, Anna, not until you're ready. But I won't deny myself the pleasure of touching you. If this is too much…" He traces the contours of my lips with a softness that steals my breath away. "Tell me to stop and I will."

I force myself to relax into his touch, and reaching up, I find the strength to lift his hand and nuzzle the soft skin of his palm. I don't know where this is going, but I need to start trusting and stop thinking, starting right now.

Holding his hand in place, I close my eyes and breathe deeply. He smells of musk and something stronger, a potent scent that calls to my blood and sets my pulse to pounding. On instinct and without thinking, I kiss his palm, his fingers, one by one until I reach his index finger and clamp my lips around it. I lift my gaze to his, watching him watching me as I suck the slim shaft slowly.

Tyler growls, a low deep sound that sets my blood on fire. He slides his finger from my mouth and begins to trail it wetly across my jaw, my throat, his tongue darting out as his lips bed down across my own in a rhythm as old as time itself.

His kiss is stoking a desire in me that, until I met him, I had no idea even existed. With a longing sigh, I wilt into him.

The kiss intensifies, his tongue thrusting deeper, demanding more. I wrap around it and lap greedily. God! I want him.

He peels his lips from mine, and I moan dejectedly. With a small chuckle, he rests his forehead against my own, his strong fingers cradling my neck as his dark eyes brand me.

"Lesson one." He kisses my nose softly, and I giggle at the absurdity if it all.

'What? How to tongue?" I ask.

"No. How to trust. I mean you no harm, Anna."

He releases me, and we exit the car hand in hand onto the wet, cold tarmac.

"My jet is at your disposal, Anna, as am I."

Fuck! Does he own his own jet?

My jaw drops, and he pushes it back up with a soft

thumb and a chuckle. "Come." He takes my passport, and along with his own, he hands them over to his driver. Mark tips his hat, and Tyler pulls me up the steps and into a world of opulence I had no idea even existed until now.

"What about your car?" I ask as he sits down beside me.

"All taken care of."

The door closes just as Mark jumps into the cabin and walks toward a curtained area at the front of the plane. I arch an eyebrow questioningly.

"Will he fly the plane as well?"

Tyler smiles and shakes his head. "No. Mark is only giving me the privacy I require. You have much to learn, little Anna. I look forward to teaching you."

I bite my lip and look away from that intense gaze he exercises so freely. I have a feeling that educating me will have nothing to do with books. Nothing at all. I close my eyes and try to catch up on the sleep he deprived me of earlier.

He wakes me up as we land, and for the next thirty minutes or so, my hand again cosseted safely within his, Tyler escorts me through the formalities of passport control and out into yet another expensive looking car. I look at the car's clock. It's only 8 a.m. here. I blink my confusion and Tyler squeezes my hand softly.

"You okay, Anna?"

"Yip. Just trying to get my head around the time difference."

He nods and looks out of his window. "We need to make a quick stop. Do you have your bank card with you?"

"Why?"

"I want confirmation that your money has been transferred."

I blink stupidly. I'd forgotten all about the auction. "Oh…okay. How much should I be looking for?"

"Two point seven million."

Fuck! He doesn't even blanch. "Dollars?"

"Sterling."

"You're shitting me."

"I never joke about money, Anna." He leans to the side, opens a small black satchel and extracts a stapled document. "I had these drawn up last night. If there is anything you wish to change, please mark and note, and we can discuss it tonight. If not…sign."

I take the document and pen from his hand and sign where the yellow sticky note points.

He looks at me like I have lost my mind and scowls.

"You should always read what you sign, Anna."

"Why? I trust you to keep your word not to hurt me, what else do I need to know?"

He gazes at me for the longest time. I flush beetroot, lower my eyes, and pick at my nails nervously.

"Please don't do that."

"What?"

"Hide your feelings in self-mutilation for one. Mark! Can you pull over please?"

The car glides to a halt beside an ATM in the cleanest little town I have ever seen.

I shake my head. "Honestly...I trust you. Please, can we just get to where we're going?"

He curses and demands my card and number.

I hand it over and mumble the pin, watching as he jumps from the car and pushes my card into the machine's slot. Minutes later, he is back in the car with a print out which he drops into my lap without ceremony.

"Read it! And don't ever assume that everyone is as honest as I am again."

I crumple the paper into a ball in my palm, and toss it out of the window.

Tyler mumbles a few choice profanities under his breath and slams himself back into his seat with animalistic energy.

The car glides out into the traffic again, and my phone rings.

I glance at him apologetically, but he isn't looking at me.

"Steph! I'm sorry. I know…I promise…okay. Love you too. 'Bye." I stuff the phone back in my pocket and glance at Tyler. "That was Steph."

"Does she know about our arrangement?"

"No, and I would prefer she didn't."

"You have no choice in the matter, Miss Wright. The contract you just signed so blindly contains a non-disclosure clause."

"I didn't sign it blindly."

"Forgive me if I disagree."

The car pulls into a tree lined drive and for several minutes we travel in anger fueled silence until I just can't take it anymore.

"What age are you, Mr. Kane?"

"What the hell has my age got to do with anything?"

"Can you just answer the damn question!"

"Fine! Thirty-four. I'm thirty-four years old, okay?" His tone is glacial.

"Then start acting like it and grow the hell up!"

The car glides to a stop in front of a house bigger than good old Queen Elizabeth's, and without preamble or apology, Tyler takes my hand in his and wrenches me from the car. "I'm going to make you wish you had never said that, Miss Wright."

He enters the house like a tornado, towing me after him through a hallway Scarlett O'Hara would have been proud to grace her hooped skirts with.

I gape in wide-eyed awe at the splendor he is pulling me through.

"Jenna! I'm in my private quarters. Do not disturb me unless the house is on fire." He leads me forward at a relentless pace through a two-story library that has me itching to stop and explore, a cavernous music room complete with grand piano and a dizzying array of guitars, and last but by no means least, into what I am assuming is to be my bedroom. Swinging me in front of him now, he kicks the heavy mahogany door deftly shut behind him.

Without pausing for breath, he pushes me to land butt down on a large four-poster bed.

Surprisingly, I'm not afraid. Just disappointed that this is the first room Tyler is introducing me to when there are so many others to explore. I remind myself that I am his to do with as he wants and force myself to sit still.

Tyler kicks off his shoes, removes his waistcoat, and pulls his shirt over his head, his gaze smoldering.

"Is this...it?" I whisper, drinking in his perfectly sculpted body.

He smiles darkly. "Lesson number two, Anna. When I say *now,* you do as I command without question. *Now.* Flip over onto all fours. Do it." His voice is low, and all the more dangerous sounding for it.

Oh, Jesus. I swallow past the adrenaline that's coursing through me and flip over and up onto all fours. I never knew my heart could beat so fast! Oh, sweet Lord.

"Lesson two?" I squeak, trying to keep the tremor from my voice and failing miserably.

I hear the hiss of his fly opening. Then the bed dips and Tyler positions himself on his knees behind me.

"Lesson three," he states, "don't say anything unless I give you permission. Nod if you understand."

I nod and bite my lips to keep my traitorous tongue still. My heart is thudding like a jackhammer, and yes, I admit it, I am a little scared, and a lot turned on, my sex thrumming with heat.

I groan and wriggle, trying to ease the building pressure within me and am awarded a hard, stinging slap that rocks me forward on my knees. Surprisingly, the pain accelerates the thrum of deliciousness within me, and I whimper.

"I am going to dry spank you for every instance you have disobeyed me, Anna. At your flat, you made me wait. Unacceptable!" I feel the brutal slap of his hand against my cheeks again, only this time, his hand stays, his fingers cupping and digging and kneading through the material of my jeans into my butt before sliding down to the back of my thighs. I moan and the pressure inside of me threatens to erupt.

"You refused to read your bank statement, and you signed my contract blindly. Unacceptable." He slaps me fiercely across my thighs. Tears spring to my eyes and drip onto my face, but not from pain. Oh no. I'm crying because the want within me is agonizing.

The bed dips and his weight vanishes from behind me. With an almost inhuman will, I force myself not to look at him, keeping my face down as instructed.

I listen to the pull of material against flesh and bite my lip again, feeling the saltiness of my own sweat as it drips into my mouth.

"Turn around, Anna. Sit on the edge of the bed. You may look at me, but do not speak."

I do as I am told, scrambling to the edge of the bed

and assuming the required position before I look up at him. My eyes widen in shock. I have never seen a man's erection before so I have nothing to compare it too, but I suddenly understand the saying "hung like a horse." He is standing gloriously naked before me, his maleness bobbing erotically in front of my face.

I watch eagerly as his hand glides up and down the silky shaft, not even close to encasing its massive length and girth.

Licking my lips, I gaze up at him hotly, awaiting his command.

He arches back, and I feel the silkiness of him brushing against my mouth.

"Open up, baby. Lesson four. Oral."

I willingly do as I am told, and he places his hands into my hair, gripping tight, positioning me.

"I'm going to fuck that little smart mouth of yours, Anna. Hard. And you will swallow everything I give you. This is your punishment."

With those final words, he bucks forward into my waiting mouth.

Acting on nothing but instinct, I close my lips around him, gripping tightly as he rams deep, the tip of his erection kissing my tonsils. Swallowing down a gag, I inhale and slide my tongue around him. I want to explore and taste every glorious ridge and soft silky dip. I want it all.

"Fuck! Anna!" He hisses, his fists tightening their grip of my hair and pulling painfully. But I don't care. That I could have this effect on such a man is empowering. He pulls back, and I suck him right back in, watching him as he trembles before me. "Slower baby," he scolds, and I feel a surge of power the likes of which I have never felt before. I sheathe my teeth and suck him in slowly, hollowing out my cheeks as I travel up and down his length, my tongue circling his girth and pushing into the small eye nestled at his tip.

His breathing accelerates with every dip of my tongue into the tight little opening, and I store the information away for future reference. He moans loudly and pushes deeper, his back arched, head thrown back.

I suck in again, harder this time, snaking my tongue around him. His head rolls forward, heated gaze fixated upon my own. "That's it, baby. Take it all." He pants erotically, and flexing his glorious hips, he begins to piston in and out of my mouth with unmerciful speed.

God, he tastes so good. I groan my pleasure against him, and he cries out, his hands gripping my head as he bucks hard and long into my lapping mouth, the tip of his cock jerking spasmodically against the back of my throat as he lets go, his body rigid. He pulls out slightly, a feral grunt tumbling from his lips before he rams my mouth again, his semen rushing across my throat. I push past my gag reflex and swallow until my throat is raw with the saltiness of his orgasm. Watching him come undone like this, the feel of him still deep within my mouth...*Ahhh, fuck*! My sex clenches, dips, and I moan in abject pleasure at the heat building within me.

Tyler quickly withdraws from my mouth and pushes me back, hard. I fall onto the bed, struggling to get my feet beneath me again as the pressure within me swells to almost painful heights. *Jesus! What's happening to me?*

He tugs at the button of my jeans, tearing them from me and throwing them to the floor.

God, I'm on fire. My head arches back into the bed. Jesus! I'm panting for him like a bitch in fucking heat!

"Not yet, Anna."

Doesn't he get it? I am not in control of this anymore. I can't stop even if I wanted to—which I don't.

The bed dips again as Tyler slides his hand inside my panties and palms my sex.

64

Biting my lip on a low moan of unparalleled pleasure, I arch up into his fingers, hissing as he inserts, first one, and then two fingers. He rotates them slowly, opening me up to him. In, out, in, picking up speed, his thumb massaging my throbbing clit. My hips circle of their own accord and he grips my chin with his free hand. "Don't move, Anna." His voice rings with authority.

"Oh, God…Tyler. Please!" I'm a quivering mess.

With a low rumble in his throat, Tyler crushes his lips to mine, his groan of pleasure wound around my tongue, fueling me on to even greater heights.

He flicks a nail tip across my clit and I stiffen beneath him.

"Come on, baby. Give it to me."

I let go, gasping for breath, my muscles bunching and tightening around his fingers, my body jerking in the throes of my orgasm.

Slipping his dripping fingers from me, Tyler pushes them into my mouth. I suck and watch as his eyes widen at the intensity of my suction.

"You are full of surprises, Miss Wright." He removes his fingers from my mouth and eases himself down onto the bed beside me.

"Lesson five, Mr. Kane?"

He smiles and slides his arm under my head. "I'm still recovering from lesson one through four, baby."

I peek up at him, my cheeks still awash with heat from my climax.

His dark hair is tousled and sexy, his body and face coated with a fine layer of sweat. His breathing is as labored as my own, his heart pounding beneath my palm.

"Did I do okay?"

He looks at me, his eyes dark and profoundly deep. Of all his features, it is his eyes I am most attracted to and aroused by.

"Beyond expectation, Miss Wright. Feel."

He pushes against me, and I gasp. His cock is rock-hard against my thigh.

I moan wantonly. God, how can I want him so much so soon after…I flush at the memory and bite my tongue. I drift my fingers across his chest, waist, across the glorious V to the soft curling hair that frames his manhood. I enclose what I can of his girth within my hand and begin to rub.

He chuckles and smacks my hand away.

"Lesson five will demand my stamina, Miss Wright, and you will need to be dressed accordingly. It's not every day I get to deflower a virgin. I want it to be the way it is in my head."

"I'm still a virgin after all of that?"

He shakes his head in amazement and pulls me upright with him.

"I am amazed that someone like you still exists, Anna. You have no idea how good that little comment makes me feel, but we have a doctor to visit and a wardrobe to plan. Come."

The rest of the day trudges by too slowly. First on the agenda is the virgin and STD tests courtesy of Tyler's private physician, Dr. Emily Reid. We are met by one of her juniors, a young man who smilingly introduces himself as Dr. Thomas McKay. He leads me into another room where I am duly pricked, prodded, and deemed fit to fuck without danger of contagion, with the added bonus of an intact hymen. I am questioned about my last period, when it started—seven days ago—and when it ended—one day ago. I am given a depo shot and Tyler is informed that no added protection will be necessary.

After a quick lunch, Tyler drives us to meet with his personal stylist, who proceeds to dress me up and down like a damn doll until I want to scream "*No more!*". This country is too hot, too humid, and too damn dusty. By the time everyone has had their little piece of me, I am near dead on my feet. I drag myself up suddenly-too-high front steps and through the double doors of Tyler's home, stopping inside to stifle a yawn and regain my breath.

Tyler snakes a welcome arm around my waist.

"Spending money is not as much fun as I thought it would be." I stifle another yawn.

He strokes my back, and without preamble, bundles me up into his arms and carries me up to bed.

I'm asleep before I even know which bed he has laid me in.

*

TYLER

He had just broken every rule he had ever lived by. The thought sat uncomfortably in Tyler's gut, but no matter how hard he tried, he couldn't bring himself to regret what had happened between them. The way she had sucked on his cock! Sweet Lord! He had experienced the pleasures of many women over the years. But no one—heaven help him—had ever sucked him off like that before. For that pleasure alone, Anna Wright deserved the treat of having his arms around her, even if she had broken a few ground rules along the way. The fact that he liked her in his arms, well, that bothered him. But he wouldn't think about it tonight, he was just too fucking tired. He lay Anna down in a bed large enough to hold five of her small frame, slipped off her shoes, and covered her with the throw from the occasional chair beside the bed.

He watched her sleeping for a moment, the urge to curl up beside her almost overwhelming.

He scowled and slapped the unfamiliar impulse back into whatever dark little hole it had crawled from. Shit! This type of thinking was dangerous. Time to shut it down before anyone got hurt. Anna Wright was an amusing novelty, nothing more.

So, what's the harm in breaking a few rules then, Ty?

He frowned. He had never shared his bed before. But then he had never acted on good old animal attraction, either. Seems Anna Wright was a first in many things for him.

She stirred in her sleep, a soft smile tilting up the corners of her mouth. Was she thinking of him? His heart did a mule kick against his rib cage, and he gave up. He gave up trying to deny what had been staring him in the face from that first accursed second, he had set eyes on her in that damned bar. He wanted Anna Wright any way he could get her, and if that meant breaking a few self-imposed rules along the way, then so be it. He had four weeks. Four weeks to fuck the girl out of his system and chalk the whole experience up to his *been there, done that, wore the fucking T-shirt* list.

Re-covering Anna with the fallen throw, he leant in and kissed her forehead. Then standing wearily, he closed the door on her sleeping form and treaded back toward his own quarters, thoughts of this morning and the delectable Miss Wright lodged firmly in mind.

It was going to be a long night.

HE HAD GIVEN UP on any form of sleep. Not with the girl who had sucked his cock so magnificently sleeping three doors down. He stared at the screen of his laptop. It stared back. "Shit." Raking his fingers through his hair he shoved it from him. What the hell was wrong with him? He couldn't work, he couldn't sleep, and he had had a fucking hard-on since Anna Wright fell on her luscious, plump butt at his feet.

His cock twitched hungrily against his thigh at just the thought of her, and Tyler hissed in disbelief that he could lose control like this.

A light knock against his bedroom door and his tormentor's face appeared around its edge.

"I'm sorry. I…Can I come in?"

"Is something wrong?" he asked.

Glancing shyly down at her feet, she shook her head.

He didn't believe her, but he would let it slip, for now.

"I'm sorry. I shouldn't have imposed." She pushed

herself away from the doorjamb with a tap of her fingers against wood.

"You haven't," he replied, not wanting her to go and hating himself for it. "I was just finishing up some work. Come in." He threw back the quilt and patted the bed in invitation for her to join him, thankful that he had opted for low-slung bottoms instead of his usual nothing.

She paused for a second, then ran across the room and jumped in beside him.

"You're freezing." He scowled, pulling the coverlet up around her.

"Sorry! One of the traits of being a vegetarian—cold feet, cold hands."

Ahhh! The light bulb popped on in his head—the restaurant. She wasn't being difficult at all. She just didn't eat meat, fish or otherwise.

"If I had known you were vegetarian, Anna, I would have ordered accordingly at the restaurant," he scolded.

She gasped in mock shock. "You mean to say it didn't mention my dietary preferences in your snoop report?"

"Remind me to fire my IT staff in the morning." He snorted through a smile. Damn! When was the last time he had shared a joke with a woman other than his housekeeper? It felt good, maybe too good. Time to change the subject.

He leaned to his left and withdrew a folder from his bedside drawer. "I have some homework for you. Hand signals."

"Hand signals?" She took the folder from him and flipped it open.

"I paid for the privilege of training you, Anna, and I intend to do just that."

Her brow knotted in concentration as she poured over the words printed beside the pictures.

"Is there anything there you don't understand?" he asked when her silence became too much to bear.

"It keeps mentioning 'point.' What is it?"

How to explain it without showing her? Tyler couldn't so—

Sliding from the bed, he held his hand out to her. "May I show you?"

After a slight pause, she took his hand and scrambled out of bed to sit on her heels at his feet. He groaned inwardly. She was a natural submissive. And she had no idea, none at fucking all. God, he was going to enjoy training Anna Wright. His cock twitched in agreement, and with great difficulty on his part, he ignored it.

"If you were in my dungeon right now—"

"You have a dungeon?" She gasped.

He lifted his hand, fingers closed all except for one, which he pointed upwards. "This symbol means?" he cocked an eyebrow and was pleased when Anna's cheeks flushed with heat. She was turned on. The thought pleased him immensely.

"Listen. Don't speak," she stated.

"Good girl." God, she was so fucking innocent! How could he take that away from her? *Because if you don't, someone else will, Ty, my boy*. The thought of anyone else touching her, pleasing her. Fuck!

"Tyler?"

He shook his head and directed his attention back to her. Anna was still sitting on her heels in the submissive position, her head raised, her eyes on his face.

An almost overwhelming need to punish her surged its way through his veins. He had spent years shutting out any form of emotion, and now this slip of a young woman was making him feel things he hadn't felt in years. Things he didn't want to feel, ever!

"You will address me as Master," he growled, flicking out a finger and drawing a Z in the air.

For a millisecond, she hesitated, her brow knotted

as her brain tried to compute what the symbol meant. "May I stand, Master?"

Pride in her overwhelmed his anger. He nodded. "You may stand, Anna. But do not undress. I want that pleasure. Lift up your arms and lower your gaze."

She unfolded herself from her crouch and did as he had directed. His cock lengthened in appreciation, and she gasped, innocent green eyes widening as his erection pushed the cotton of his bottoms away from his body.

"Not yet, little Anna." He chuckled. "But I will reward you and show you just what your splendid submission is doing to me right now." He removed his bottoms and stepped forward, the tip of his erection brushing against the denim of her jeans as he slid her top up over her shoulders, arms, and neck. Her eyes he left covered, leaving only the small stub of her nose and parted lips on display. "I want you to trust me, Anna. Do you trust me?" He trailed a hand over her neck, relishing the tremor that ran through her wherever his touch fell. "Answer me, Anna." He breathed softly against her neck, his fingers pushing the wire of her bra beneath her breast, pushing the hard points of her breasts even higher.

Damn, but she was beautiful.

"Yes. And no, Master," she replied with quickened breaths.

"Then I shall have to persuade you, little Anna." He lowered his mouth and rolled the hard point of a nipple between his teeth. Anna groaned and reached for him.

He stepped back and placed her hands gently at her side again. "What we are doing right now is called a scene, Anna. During a scene, you will not touch me without my permission. If you do, I will punish you. If you wish me to stop, if things become too ... intense, just say the word '*black*', and I will stop. Do you understand?"

She licked her lips and balled her hands. "Yes, Master."

"I am going to finish undressing you now. Do not move unless I tell you to."

Slipping to his knees, he gripped her waistband and tugged hard. She jerked forward but did not touch him. "Good girl, Anna. You learn fast. I like that. I like that a lot." Grabbing the denim, he slid it slowly from her skin, enjoying the feel of her beneath his fingers. Her breaths were quick and fast now, her arousal obvious. He wanted to taste that arousal, feel it on his tongue, savor it like the mighty fine thing it was.

Fisting the flimsy material of her panties, he ripped them free. "Open up to me, baby." She immediately parted her legs, her breath an erratic pant, her breasts rising and falling rapidly in her excitement.

His sac tightened at the sound, and with a low groan, he latched onto her mound, parting her with his tongue. Fuck! She was soaking, her clit bulging. He flicked the needy little rosette with his tongue, and she mewled. He flicked again, and again, circling, licking, nipping, and she screamed, head arched back as she orgasmed, her hands fisting in his hair. He removed his mouth with a final lick and stood up. Anger that he had pleased her and she had repaid him with disobedience surged through his veins. She needed to be punished.

"On your hands and knees, Anna."

Still panting, she dropped onto all fours, and he ripped the top from her eyes.

He needed a belt. No. Not a belt—something milder—his palm. He rummaged through his brain. Trying to think if he had soothing cream on hand, and after a few seconds of second-guessing himself, he marched into his bathroom and emptied the vanity unit in one swift sweep of his hand. A small bottle of cream lay amongst the rubble. Tyler snatched it up and padded barefoot back into his bedroom. She was still on her hands and knees, eyes down, panting.

"Anna. Look at me."

She lifted her gaze and locked it with his.

"Say my name."

"Tyler, Master."

"You need to be punished, Anna. Do you understand?"

"No, Master, I don't," she stated.

He almost buckled then. Almost but not quite. She had asked for this when she had sold herself to the highest bidder. She had asked for it the moment she had fisted his hair during her orgasm. The rules were very simple. Now it was his job to teach her how reckless that act had been. This was for her as much as it was him. Maybe even more so.

"Then it is my job to ensure you do understand. I am going to spank you, Anna. I will slap you four times with my palm. You will not cry out, and you will count off each, and every slap. If you do cry out, Anna, I will add another four slaps to your tally. When I am finished, you will thank me and assume whatever position I command you. Do you understand?"

"Yes, Master." Her voice had taken on a steelier

tone, and he mentally applauded her.

"I want you to assume, for this scene, that this is *point*—this spot in my room is *point,* Anna. If I say that word, you will come to this exact spot, and assume the position you are in now. Now. Stand up."

She stood compliantly while he lowered himself to sit on the edge of the bed, his erection almost painful now. "Lie chest down across my knees, Anna, feet planted on the ground, slightly apart, bum high."

She did as she was told and he had to fight the desire not to fuck her right there and then. Inhaling sharp and deep, Tyler waited until he was in full control again. Then opened his eyes.

Anna's butt rose high on his right side. On his left, large aroused nipples brushed against his thighs, and long brunette hair trailed down her back. He fisted that hair tightly, holding her in place as he brought his open palm down hard enough to welt. She whimpered but did not scream.

After a second's hesitation, she stated shakily, "One, Master."

His cock jerked, brushing a nipple, and she gasped. He bit down a groan of delight and, leaning low, traced his tongue along the apex of her cheeks, down towards her sex, poking once, twice inside. Then withdrawing quickly, he slapped her again, just below those damn beautiful cheeks. The force rocked her forward, his grip in her hair the only thing stopping her from falling. Without waiting to see her reaction, Tyler cupped her sex firmly and slipped three fingers inside her, careful to keep the movement shallow. She was soaking wet. *Fuck!* Withdrawing his hand, he slapped her again, softer this time, and kneaded the reddened flesh gently. Then raising his hand again, Tyler slapped her, hard, right below that delightfully haired mound.

She hissed out, "Four, Master. Thank you, Master." Her face was wet with tears as he pulled her hair back, forcing her to slide from his knees to the ground at his feet. He smiled, his anger dissipated.

"Relax now, baby. How was that for you?"

She lifted her gaze and blinked. Jesus! His breath caught in his throat at that look. Anna Wright, the girl he had brought all the way from Scotland just so he could deflower her, looked like a doe caught in the headlights of a car.

"Anna?"

"Is it always like that?" she asked. Too quietly.

Tyler patted the bed beside himself, and Anna gingerly pushed herself up and sat with a wince and a hiss at his side. "Lie on your tummy, baby. I have cream that can help with the sting."

She shook her head lightly, but lay down anyway, large eyes bright in a face that was too pale.

He grabbed the soothing cream and squirted a liberal amount onto his palm, warming it before applying. His handprints stood out red on Anna's skin. He had meant to educate her, but instead, he had punished her. His erection flopped against his thigh, thick, warm and consigned to the corner for a time out. "No, Anna." He soothed the cream across the welts as gently as he could, taking note of the scars that crisscrossed in ugly white lines across her back. He would ask about them in the morning. She had enough to process tonight without him overcomplicating things for her.

"It's not always like that. The pain is counterbalanced with pleasure until the two become one. Do you understand?"

She nodded and winced as his hand massaged the delicate skin below the apex where her thighs gave way to the fleshier part of her cheeks. Full round cheeks with just the right amount of wobble. His erection raised its head in hope as an image of vibrating butt plugs flashed across his warped mind.

81

Getting way ahead of yourself here, Tyler. She's still a virgin for fuck's sake. Slow it down, dickhead. Or you'll lose her respect before you even begin.

With great difficulty, he tore his gaze away from that deliciously tight little orifice, and onto her face.

"I was turned on," she confessed in a whisper, eyes closed tight, cheeks flushed with…what? Embarrassment?

Laying the cream aside, he flipped her gently around to face him. "And that emotion embarrassed you, Anna?"

"I don't know, Ty—"

She hesitated, lips trembling.

"Baby, when you're off point or I say relax—then I'm Tyler again. Just Tyler and you can tell me anything. I won't be embarrassed, and I won't judge."

She sat up, chin on knees, and he could see from her expression that she was deliberating whether she could trust him or not.

Baby, I'm the only person in the world you can trust with this shit, his mind scoffed. He had enough secrets for both of them. Maybe if he shared one with her. *No*, his mind screamed. *Are you insane? She's a fucking sub, Ty. Treat her like one!* He pushed his thoughts aside with a resigned sigh.

"I have been where you are now, Anna. It's confusing, isn't it? On the one hand, you feel degraded, used, dirty, but on the other—that feeling of freedom your arousal provides you with is breathtakingly beautiful, is it not? You were turned on because pain and pleasure are one and the same thing, Anna."

She shook her head miserably. "I don't understand any of this shit, Tyler. I just d…"

He had to rescue this. Now. He was so not ready to say goodbye to little Miss Anna Wright yet. "Lie down, Anna. Let me show you how the two are combined, baby."

"I'm not on point, Tyler. You can't order me about now." Her eyes flashed a peculiar aquamarine that affected his cock in the most spectacular way. He stood up and his cock sprang forward, his sac tightening in anticipation of what was coming. And as he knew she would, she lay down, eyes flitting feverishly between his face and his erection. With a slow sensual grin, he slid his hands up her legs, nose skimming along her inner thigh until he reached his goal, and locked on, teasing her with tugging kisses until she was a panting mess.

"Tyler, please." She whimpered.

"Patience, baby. I want you to feel the pleasure, and

83

the pain."

Anna's fists grabbed at the sheets in desperation, and Tyler smiled.

"Not yet, baby."

He inserted his thumb into her sex, stretching her in small slow circles, always careful to keep the movements shallow—her hymen was for his cock only. She mewled, and he slipped his thumb from her sex into the tight little opening he had so admired earlier. She cried out and instinctively tried to repel his thumb, but he only pushed deeper, circled, then out. In. Out. In. Out. Her yelps of pain quickly transgressed over to gasping groans of pleasure. Still, thumb-fucking her ass, he inserted his tongue deep within her sex, circling that oh-so-sweet little cherry that swelled and throbbed so deliciously beneath his expert tongue. Flicking his tongue faster, he fanned her desire to fantastical heights, his thumb still deep within that deliciously tight little opening, pushing against the inner walls toward her sex. He added a finger to his thumb, slowly teasing her open as he thrust in and out, deeper and faster, his own desire throbbing, dangerously close to letting go.

"Come on, baby," he commanded between licks, his erection beginning to bead and moisten, his sac tightening and jerking high.

"Ahhh!!" What was this girl doing to him?

She arched high, away from the bed, and he quickly scrambled to his knees, tongue deep as her clit dipped frantically against his tongue, soaking it with sweet, fresh moisture. She screamed his name, and that was all it took. Just his name in the throes of her orgasm and he exploded in spurts of hot, warm moisture that left him breathless and spent.

Jesus H. Christ! He lifted his head and blinked at her in shock, her look of amazement mirroring his own.

"Anna. What the fuck are you doing to me?" he whispered, amazed at the intensity of his own orgasm.

"Pleasure and pain, I think you said." She smiled brilliantly and he forgot how to breathe. God, but she was beautiful.

Sliding up beside her he pulled sheets wet with his semen around them, and spooned himself around her, his chest to her back, arms holding her tight.

This wasn't just about sex anymore. It went way deeper than that, and it scared the shit out of him.

ANNA

Sun tickles my eyes, my throat hurts, and my body feels like the wearer of a thousand bruises.

I groan and sit up gingerly, hissing as my muscles complain and spasm.

The bathroom door opens, and Tyler walks out, his face impassive, his eyes as dark as always.

I reach for a coverlet to hide my nakedness, but he shakes his head.

"Don't. I like to look at you. You are exceptional, Anna. In every way."

He walks toward a large closet and pulls out a tie and tailored black suit jacket. He slips the tie around his neck, and I sit up, wincing as pain smarts across my butt.

He hitches up his trouser legs lightly and sits at the bottom of the bed, his fingers deftly clipping his cuff links into place.

"There are scars on your back. How did they get there?"

I wince at the casualness of his tone and drop my gaze.

Seconds tick into minutes before he speaks again.

"If you had read our contract, Anna, you would have realized that honesty, at all times, *on both sides,* is non-negotiable. Now, the scars?"

I take a deep breath, hold, then let it all out. "Is it also in your damn contract that I need permission to dress? Or would you prefer I answer your questions naked and on my knees? Sir!"

He purses his lips and looks at me with a spark of fire in those dark, dark eyes. "I have laid your clothes out in my dressing room."

"Which is where exactly?"

He marches forward, and yanks open the door to my right.

"Some of your new outfits are in here. The rest will be delivered this afternoon. Underwear and toiletries are in the units beneath the rails. The outfit I want you to wear today is on the chaise lounge in the corner. There." He nods toward the far end of the dressing room and the clothes that he has chosen for me to wear. Then he straightens his tie.

87

"Unfortunately, as I didn't expect *you* to happen, I haven't scheduled time for you into my diary. I will amend that shortly, but in the intervening time between that happening and now, you are free to do as you wish. Within reason. My housekeeper, Mrs. Greene, and her husband will be on hand should you need anything."

I nod and walk past his stiff formality with a begrudging smile. How can he be so fucking cold after everything that happened between us last night? *Because he doesn't care for you, honey,* bitches my inner voice. *You're here to appease his sexual needs, Anna. Nothing more.*

"Thank you." I smile, injecting the words with just a tad too much sweetness for sincerity.

"My pleasure, Anna, and while you dress, you can tell me what happened to scar you like that."

Bastard doesn't give up, does he, snipes my inner voice. *Tell him to go fuck himself. It's none of his damned business.*

As much as I am tempted to heed that snide little voice in my head, I ignore it and wrap myself in the beautiful lacy underwear he has chosen for me. Bending my leg up onto the chaise, I attach a stocking with deliberate slowness before I answer, taking satisfaction in the lustful hunger that drips from him like liquid candy.

"My parents were sick, twisted individuals, who got their kicks out of looking for new ways to hurt their kids, Mr. Kane. The scars on my back were inflicted after two days in a dark under-stair cupboard with no food or water. My wee brother was in there with me. He wasn't moving and I—" I close my eyes as emotions long buried flare to life within me. I will not lose it here. Not in front of him. I won't give Tyler Kane the satisfaction of seeing me so damned weak. Snapping my eyes open, I continue with steel in my voice. "I couldn't wake him up."

I yank a pale green silk shift dress over my head. "I can't reach this zip...Would you mind?"

I pull my hair up and secure it with a large clip. Tyler walks brusquely forward, zips me up, then steps back.

"What age was your brother, Anna?" His voice is cold and full of steel, and oddly, I take strength from it.

I sit down and leaning forward suggestively, I slip my feet into the delicate jade heels. The action allows me the opportunity to direct his attention away from my face and onto my cleavage. I don't want to see pity in his eyes when I tell him what happened next.

"He was eighteen months old."

"Anna…"

I cut across his apologetic plea. I don't want his damn apology. He dragged this up, and I'm going to fucking finish it.

"Seems my lovely parents broke one of his ribs before locking us in that damn cupboard. A piece of bone fragment had pierced his left lung. He was dead before they turned the key." I wipe warm tears from my cheeks and stop to gather some semblance of order over my voice before I continue. "And there wasn't a damn thing I could do about it."

Silence meets my words, and when I look past my hair again, I am alone in the dressing room. I drop my head into my arms and cry until I have no tears left to cry.

Thirty minutes have passed before I find the strength to lift myself up off the floor and discard the clothing Tyler chose for me to wear. I re-dress in an outfit better suited to my own tastes and walk out of the closet towards Tyler's overly large bed, indecision in my every step.

The last thing I want to do is leave this room to explore, but the thought of staying here and feeling sorry for myself doesn't do it for me, either.

I hover for several seconds and then grab my phone and purse, leaving Tyler's room intent on spending some of the money that is lying static in my bank account.

I head down the corridor with its fabric-decorated walls and cream carpet. It's the grandest hallway I have ever walked down. Not that I've walked down many—I'm more of a corridor-walking girl.

I stop to admire a large canvas on the wall above the staircase. It's Madame Monet and child, and it's either a very accurate reproduction or the real thing.

"Ah, I see you've noticed my old friend Madame—"

"Monet," I whisper in awe and turn to find a middle-aged woman wearing a huge smile and balancing a washing basket on her ample hips.

"You know Monet's work?" she enquires in a charming Southern accent.

I return her smile and relieve her of the heavy-looking basket of laundry.

"Not personally, just from course work and books. This is a beautiful reproduction."

I fall into step beside the woman I suspect is Tyler's housekeeper, Mrs. Greene.

"If you say so, honey."

"You mean it's the *real Monet*?"

She opens the heavy door before us and takes the basket from me.

"I never said that, Miss Wright. Those are your words."

"Please, my name is Anna. Can I help you with anything?" I ask as she struggles to place the large basket down without dislocating her hips.

She looks at me quizzically, her grey caterpillar eyebrows meeting in the middle.

"Honestly, I don't have anything to keep me occupied so if I can help..."

"Well, I do need some bits and bobs from Slowpokes, if you're sure?"

"Slowpokes?" Who names a shop Slowpokes? I fight to keep a straight face and nod.

"Okay, just tell me what you need and point me in the right direction."

"Tyler left you a set of keys to the Cherokee. It's in the garage. You go get yourself acquainted with it while I finish this off and get you that list."

"Okay, sounds like a plan. Erm..." I look around in confusion. "Which way is the garage?"

"Sorry, honey. I forget how confusing this house is

when you're not used to it." She chuckles and points me in the right direction.

I thank her, and true to my word, ten minutes later, I am pumping the left-hand drive car's accelerator and smiling like the proverbial Cheshire cat from Alice Land. "Man, I need to get myself one of these." The thing is huge. A *fuck off and don't mess with me* Jeep that promises, *I will crush you to glitter if you so much as even think of jumping those lights before me dude, bitch—hell, I don't care what you are! Just don't go there!* I stroke the wheel in amazement that I'm actually going to get to drive it.

"Anna!"

I stick my head out of the window, not quite willing to leave this beautiful specimen of a car yet.

"Aye?"

"Here's that list of groceries I need. I've let the boys at the gatehouse know you're on your way down, so just drive right on through, honey."

She hands me a lined list with curly lavender writing, her breathing slightly labored.

"When you get to the T-junction at the bottom, turn left, or you'll end up at the lake.

I nod and take the list from her. "Mrs. Greene, are you okay?"

93

"Just too much good living catching up with me, Anna honey. I'll be right as rain after a scone and a mug of coffee or two. Definitely, two. Now go already!"

I grin and tentatively move forward. The accelerator is sensitive, the gearbox clunky, but that's just my driving. Every car I drive feels like this so I push it into second, third, fourth, and the gatehouse zooms past.

At the bottom of the drive, I turn left as directed. It feels like I'm maneuvering a dumper truck. I try to relax, telling myself that even I couldn't crash this lovely specimen of heavy engineering.

Twenty minutes later, I discover that Slowpokes is, indeed, a real place, complete with everything from coiled ropes, cable ties, and sacks of rice to slush puppies. I bite my lip in concentration, and fish Mrs. Greene's list from my jeans pocket.

A young girl wearing an apron three sizes too big for her and an over the top smile springs kangaroo-style in my direction.

"Welcome to Slowpokes, miss. What can I get for you today?"

I hand her the list and grimace apologetically.

She nods and scans the list. "This is for Mrs. Greene

94

up at the big house?"

"Aye. How did you know?"

"She's the only one in this town who uses lilac ink to write her list. How is she?"

"Um, fine, I think. I don't really know her all that well yet."

Little Miss Kangaroo picks up a basket, and I follow behind, noting where everything is for future reference.

"You the foreigner that Mr. Kane brought home with him then?"

I grimace. "It didn't take long for the rumor mill to churn, did it?"

The young girl smiles an honest-to-God smile and sticks her hand out past the half-filled basket.

"You'll get used to it. A town this small, there really ain't much else to do but gossip. My names Bonnie Ray, by the way."

I take her hand and shake. "Anna Wright. This your family's store?"

"Yeah. Dad makes me work weekends. He says it's character building." She pulls a face and grabs a pack of toilet rolls from the shelf.

"I take it you don't see it that way?"

She grunts and rolls her eyes. "I know Dad means

well, but…you know."

I nod in sympathy and pull out my purse as the list nears its end.

"So…" She rounds the large wooden counter top and begins to tally up the goods. "You going to be here for a while then?"

"You fishing, Bonnie?"

She flashes me what I suspect is her best twen-ty-watt grin. "Hell yeah! Mr. Kane has *never* brought anyone home with him before. We all thought he was…you know…one o' those homosexual types."

Oh, if you only knew, little Bonnie! "Maybe he is…I can't comment. I'm only here on business, and Mr. Kane was good enough to invite me to stay with him until my business is concluded. You can tell all the ladies not to worry. He's still on the market, and I'll be returning back to Scotland in a couple of weeks."

"I knew it! Just wait until I tell Gail I met you. She'll be green with envy that I met you first. She's got a real thing for Mr. Kane. Hell! Every woman, girl, and maybe even some of those guys that visit the old lake house would give their right arms to be in your shoes right now!"

"And what about you, Bonnie. Are you a fan of Tyler's as well?" I smirk.

"Honestly, Miss?" She looks me up and down in open appreciation and grins. "My papa would kill me if he knew I said this but I prefer looking at you."

I should be shocked, but after the events of the past week, I don't think anything will ever shock me again. I chuckle and take the groceries the slim girl with the mischievous twinkle in her eyes holds out to me.

"How much for this Bonnie?"

"I've added it to the house account. The receipt is in the bag. Tell Mrs. Greene and Mr. Thomas that Bonnie said hi."

"Will do. It was a pleasure talking to you, Bonnie."

"Likewise, Anna. Call back anytime."

So, this is what a small American town feels like—a goldfish bowl with smiles, glances, and whispers.

I place Mrs. Greene's shopping into the front passenger seat beside me and flick on the radio. Bruno Mars blares out in stereo as I pull away from the curb, studiously ignoring every face that plants itself against the glass of shop fronts or stops with a curious glance on their faces at my passing.

"Homosexual." I laugh aloud. Wait until I tell Tyler. And then I remember what happened earlier, and my black mood returns with a sledgehammer against my heart.

I drive the Cherokee into an empty space outside of a shop whose window displays an impressive array of lawnmowers of all things, and pulling out my phone, I call Steph.

She answers on the fifth ring, her voice slurred with sleep.

"This had better be fucking good!"

"Steph. It's Anna."

"It's the middle of the friggin' night here, Anna!"

"Sorry...I never thought, I'll call—"

"Oh, no, you don't! Now that you've woken me up, you had better fill me in. I've been worried sick about you!"

"I'm sorry. Did I wake up Frank?"

"Frank's over *there,* Anna. Which you would have known if you had phoned me earlier!"

"Steph—" My voice wobbles and I shut my traitorous mouth.

"Anna? You okay?"

"Yes. No. I had a fight with his lordship."

Silence and then— "Anna, I know about the deal you and Tyler have going on. Frank chewed him out big time when Tyler let slip why you were over there with him. For God's sake, Anna, what were you thinking?

Tyler's hot and all, but selling him your virginity? Jesus."

"Don't Steph. Please just … don't. You're not saying anything I haven't told myself." Silence. A heavy sigh. Then—

"So, tell me what the big fight with his lordship was about."

"He saw my scars and demanded to know how I got them."

"And you told him!" She sounds incredulous. "Anna, that shit freaked me out. Still does if I think about it, which I try not to, by the way."

More silence buzzes down the line between us.

"Hell, Anna. You're too fucking trusting. I take it he wasn't impressed?"

"I don't know. He left before I could gauge his reaction. I haven't seen him all morning."

"Where are you now?"

"I'm just leaving Grafton. Doing a little shopping."

"Okay." She sighs. "At least I know you're safe. I'll check back on you this afternoon. Okay?"

"Thanks, Steph."

"Chin up, baby girl, and don't take any more of that guy's shit. He bought your virginity, not you. He wants anything else, you tell him to go fuck himself."

I snort out a laugh, say my goodbyes, and end the call. Steph's right. I shouldn't have to tell Tyler Kane anything. And I ain't taking no more mood swinging crap from him either, no matter how hot he is. My inner self whoops and punches the air in jubilation. *About fucking time, girl!*

MRS GREENE IS IN the kitchen, hands knuckle deep in dough.

"Hey." I heft the paper bag up onto the black granite island that dominates the kitchen area. "You might have warned me I was entering gossip central." I lift an apple from the overladen fruit bowl and bite. Hard.

She chuckles. "Anna, honey, sometimes you just have to find things out for yourself. Did Bonnie get everything on the list?"

"Aye. She's a cute kid."

"Won't be for long if her papa keeps her cooped up like he does. I told him! I said *'Bill Ray! You gonna smother that girl till she can't take no more and then you'll be sorry!'* But will he listen? Oh no! Bill Ray knows better than everyone else." She huffs, pounding the dough hard. "Teenagers need an outlet, Anna. Hell! I know that better than anyone around here

100

does."

"You were a wild child, Mrs. Greene." I grin incredulously and chomp hard.

"Heck, I was *the* wild child, honey. There ain't nothing no one can teach this old mama if you catch my meaning." She winks suggestively.

"Mrs. Greene! You, dirty old dog!" I laugh.

Damn! She looks like an innocent homebody. *Lesson six, Anna! Never judge a book by its cover!*

"What about Tyler?" I ask innocently between bites.

"Oh, baby girl, I ain't getting into that one. What I will say, though, is that Tyler ain't ever brought anyone home before, and into his room too…" Mrs. Greene quirks her eyebrows and shakes her head. "Unheard of. I raised that boy as my own after his mama died, and up until now, he's kept his private life just that … private. I ain't never met any of his women. Until you. And if I know that boy like I *know* I do—he ain't gonna let you go home in a few weeks."

"You're way off, Mrs. Greene. His Lordship isn't even talking to me this morning."

She shakes her wiry curls and smiles. "You a betting lady, Anna?"

"What's the bet?" I chuckle, lifting the coffee pot from its tray.

101

"Five thousand dollars says my boy Tyler will propose to you within the coming month."

"Do I need to accept his proposal to win?" I laugh, enjoying myself for the first time since arriving here. Well, with my clothes on anyway.

"Honey, he's a billionaire and hot to boot—you'd be a fool to reject him. But in answer to your original question, no, you don't have to accept. You will! But you don't have to, is all I'm saying."

"Okay." I smirk, throwing my finished apple into the bin. "You. Are. On."

"Oh, and, Anna honey, I take checks, so keep that checkbook of yours handy. As for dinner for the next few nights—it's just me, you, Thomas, and my niece Lilith has decided to grace us with her company. I hope you don't mind eating down here with us. Tyler has some business in Saudi for the next few days. One of his fields is being inspected or something along those lines."

Disappointment that I won't get to see him tonight washes through me.

Mrs. Greene laughs and pounds the dough down hard onto the worktop. "Like I said, honey. Easy money!"

***

THE DAY FLIES BY. I explore the open rooms. Half are locked, especially on the lower level—the dungeons as Mrs. Greene nicknames them. I'm sure I'll see them soon enough. The thought depresses me, and I have no idea why.

The library is my last port of call and the best of them. It's huge, at least three stories high, with a plush green tartan carpet and forest green walls. The staircase looks like half a tree carved intricately and beautifully into bannister steps. The books themselves are protected behind etched glass cabinets that shimmer in the dying light of the day.

I spend four hours sifting through well-kept index cards until I find what I'm looking for on the first floor to the right of the fire. I open the case door slowly, my heart hammering in my chest, and softly pull out a leather bound first edition of *Jane Eyre*.

I hug it to my chest and close my eyes in sheer ecstasy. I have died and gone to heaven.

Mrs. Greene pops her head around the door. "Dinner's laid, Anna."

"Do you think Tyler would mind if I read this?" I

ask, brandishing the book toward her.

"Honey! He gave me strict instructions that you were to have the run of the house. So, read away. But dinner first. I hope you're not a faddy vegetarian freak. I don't do that kind of cooking," she warns.

"As long as there are potatoes and butter, I'm a happy bunny." And with one last stroke of Jane Eyre's cover, I lay it down on the arm of the chair I intend on occupying later, and fall into step behind Mrs. Greene's ample frame.

"I have a spare ten dollars in my pocket that say he'll call you before ten." She smirks.

"You're on." Something tells me I have just been conned. But I don't mind. I like Mrs. Greene. I like her a lot.

Dinner is huge with at least thirteen dishes laid out like a Fourth of July feast. An older man I recognize as the man who picked us up from the airport is pouring himself a beer, and a younger woman around my age, but dark and confident next to my sallow and unsure, is smiling happily and devouring a sweetcorn with relish.

She wipes her hand and sticks it out. "Sorry. It might feel a little greasy. I'm Lilith."

Mrs. Greene slaps Lilith's head. "You're a damn pig is what you are, girl. God above, I am sure they must have given ma sister the wrong baby at the maternity unit. Thomas?"

"Nope!" Thomas states matter-of-factly. "She's got your family's genetics, honey. Even got those sexy hips like you and your sister, bless her soul."

Mrs. Greene scowls and slaps potatoes onto her already overflowing plate. "Help yourself, Anna. We don't stand to attention down here. Hell…Lilith just uses her damn fingers to get what she wants."

Lilith winks at me and pulls a sticky rib out of the dish with the offending fingers.

I grin and grab a beer from the stack in the middle of the table.

"So, Anna, put us out of our misery here," mumbles Lilith through a mouthful of meat.

I gulp down a mouthful of potato and lower my fork in panic.

"Your accent…is it Irish or English?"

I laugh in nervous relief. "Neither. I'm Scottish. Glasgow to be exact."

"You owe me, you old coot. Hand it!" Lilith whoops and thrusts her hand, palm upwards, toward Tyler's amply framed housekeeper.

"Lilith, baby, I owe you nothing. You, however, owe me twenty-two long years of looking after your butt twenty-four seven."

Lilith rolls her eyes heavenwards. "Change the record, woman. You owe me, so pay up. She does this all the time, you know. When she wins, she lets you know loud and clear, but when she loses…well, you just saw it for yourself. You're a cheat, Aunt."

"Maybe so. But honey, I'm a cheat with money. Thomas, you had better get a move on, baby. I told William you'd be there around eight. Oh, and you're supposed to take some bourbon with you. Seems he's all out again." She shakes her head and mutters, "Not that he had any to begin with." Standing up, she starts to remove the plates, leaving the beers and a grand plate of hot apple pie on the table. "Dig in, girls. I want this table cleared in the next ten minutes. I got a date with a hot bath and large glass of brandy."

I look from the pie to Lilith. She shakes her head and flicks her head suggestively to the side.

I nod, and we both leave the kitchen on tiptoe.

"So, Anna, how about you and me hitting some bars in town?"

We're standing at the foot of the staircase. Lilith is

pulling on her coat, a tight little denim jacket that matches her painfully tight-looking jeans. If Steph were here she would say, Lilith gives the term *camel hoof* new meaning. I grin, and shake my head. "No can do. Sorry. I have a date with a book and a glass of Chablis in the library."

"You're passing up a night on the town to read a damn book? Seriously?" She snorts.

I nod in confusion. "Actually, yes, I am."

"Honey," she sneers, "I know you're his new sub. So, let's just cut with the bullshit."

What the hell is going on here? Unless—fuck! My eyes widen in shock, and I stumble back a step, or three. "You're one of his subs?"

"And I don't like sharing, so first thing tomorrow morning, you're gonna make your excuses and fuck off back to wherever you came from. Y'hear me?" Her tone is feral, all traces of her earlier friendliness gone.

Anger, raw and undiluted, bubbles through my veins. I didn't sign up for this shit. Not from Tyler Kane, and most certainly not from one of his crazy sub whores.

"I am not—" I shake my head and step forward into her crazy zone, "a fucking sub. His, or anyone else's. That kind of shit, Lilith, I leave to sick little whores like you."

"He needs *sick little whores* like me, honey. And when he's done playing house, I'll be the one he comes crawling back to."

"Whatever, Lilith. Go back to your kennel now. There's a good dog."

I never saw it coming. All my years on the streets, and I never saw it coming. My nose crunches under the weight of her elbow.

Damn! Seriously? I mean who the hell uses their elbow to throw a fucking punch?

Balling my fist, I punch the bitch back. Hard.

She stumbles back in shock, her eyes warier than they had been seconds before.

"What's wrong, Lilith? No one ever hit back before?"

"Fuck you, bitch."

"Nah! Fucking bitches ain't my thing, Lilith. Not when I've got an Alpha to take care of me. Now piss off, before I actually lose my temper and shove my size fives where the sun doesn't shine. Go on. Fuck off."

With flying dark hair and a nose bloodier than my own, Lilith flicks me a finger and bangs shut the front door on her nasty little ass.

"Jesus."

I slump down the bannister to the step below, wiping the blood from my nose with my sleeve. How many of Tyler's exes are out there just waiting to punch my fucking block off? Five? Ten? Twenty? Something tells me the number is much higher. I shake my head, and for the first time since I met Tyler Kane, I can't wait to see the back of him.

"Anna?"

"I'm here. Fell and hit my nose on that damn bannister," I lie.

"Sweet Lord, child." She hauls me gently to my feet and walks me into the kitchen where she places an ice pack on my nose.

"That's gonna bruise."

I nod sagely, trying very hard not to gag on the blood lumping in my throat.

"I'm gonna kill Lilith when I get my hands on her."

"I fell. Honestly."

Mrs. Greene smiles sadly. "Honey, I appreciate you trying to cover for her, but she ain't worth it. Heavens above I know that better than anyone. Lilith is my sister all over again, and she was one nasty little madam." She snorts disdainfully.

"Can I have some water please?"

She nods and is back in quick time with a glass of

water. I take the glass from her gratefully. "Thank you, Mrs. Greene. For everything, I mean."

She nods and somewhere in the background a phone rings shrilly.

Mrs. Greene pats my shoulder and smiles knowingly.

"If I don't get that, he's gonna be packing his bags quick time to come home."

I chuckle and wince simultaneously.

Mrs. Greene waddles off to get the trilling phone.

Maybe I should be packing my bags. If I didn't need the damn money so much, I would do just that.

"Anna, honey, Tyler wants a word with you."

I set down my water and take the phone from Mrs. Greene with fingers that tremble more than they should.

"Hi," I rasp.

Mrs. Greene smiles encouragingly and disappears.

"Anna?" His voice is a soft caress in my ear. I cradle the phone close and exhale that breath I have been keeping in since he left me. God, I have it bad for this guy.

"When will you be back?" I mumble miserably

"Tomorrow afternoon. Anna, I wanted to say I'm sorry."

110

I need to change the subject. Fast. That part of my life ended the day my brother died, and I have no intention of digging out that pain today, or any other day.

"I met Lilith tonight."

Silence

"She let me know exactly what she thought of me. I think she might have broken my nose."

"I'm coming home. Right now." His tone is glacial.

"To do what, Tyler? Bind me? Gag me maybe? Or better still, why don't you invite your fucking subs, and we can all have an orgy!"

"Stop it!"

"Stop what, Tyler?"

"Stop acting like this is my fault! You placed that fucking ad, Anna. Not me. You."

"Fuck. You. Tyler Kane. You know why I placed that ad, you sanctimonious prick."

"Anna—"

"Don't you dare 'Anna' me. Don't you fricking dare. This is some seriously messed up shit here, Tyler. And you! You are one seriously messed up man. Four fucking weeks, and I'm outta here, Tyler. And buy your bitch a leash. 'Cause the next time I see her, I'm going to rip her arse to fucking elbow."

I end the call before he can reply and break down into breathless wracking sobs. I can't live like this. Not for Tyler Kane. Not for anyone. I just can't.

The phone rings again, and Mrs. Greene appears like dust on the wind. One look at her, and I turn tail and sprint up into Tyler's bedroom of all bloody places.

Flopping down onto his bed, I bury my face in his pillows and cry myself to an uneasy sleep.

ANNA

Morning brings a relentless pounding in my head, a black eye, cut nose, and the hope that things can only get better. I mean, it's not like they can get much worse.

So with this in mind, I hiss my way through a shower, brush with Tyler's toothbrush—damn, I've got it bad—dress in Capri jeans and a cropped white shirt, and, last but not least, I help Mrs. Greene with her chores. By two o'clock, I'm totally whacked but happy. I jump off the ride-on mower my butt's been glued to all morning and wilt down onto sun baked steps at the back of the house. Closing my eyes, I let the warm afternoon sun bake me into one happy little cupcake—all brown on top and soft and fluffy in the middle. Lilith is past tense, so I leave her there to freeze in the darkness of my memories.

A scuffing on the steps of heavy feet and hip sway has me opening one eye. Mrs. Greene gazes back with a plate full of sandwiches and a large glass of iced water in her hands. I pat the step beside me with a welcome grin and take what she offers gratefully.

"Thank you. I needed this. Want to join me, Mrs. Greene?"

"If I could get down there and back up without having a heart attack, I would take you up on that, honey. But I can't, so eat up and bring the plate back in when you're finished."

I nod and chew until there is nothing left to chew on. Then with a full stomach, quenched thirst, and the hot sun beating down on me, I allow myself to succumb to the tiredness that had been dogging me persistently since I got here.

"Anna!"

Flipping upwards like a marionette on drugs, I check my mouth for drips and blink.

"You have a delivery, honey. Better come on in for a minute and see what it is."

In the kitchen, a large bouquet of red carnations awaits me with a box that's just as red and wrapped with a huge white bow.

No one has ever sent me flowers before. In fact, no one has ever sent me anything before. Tears come unbidden to my eyes as I retrieve the card from its foliage nest and read.

I meant what I said to you, Anna.

I will not hurt you.

Trust me, baby.

Thinking of you, as fucking always, little witch.

Tyler xx

I smile at the card like it's a living thing. Tears burn my eyes and I wipe them away before they can fall.

Uh, oh! You're falling for him, Anna. Not a good idea, baby. Not good at all.

"Shut up," I mumble into empty air. Then slipping the ribbons from around the box, I open its lid.

Inside is a delicate yet sturdy silver chain, intricately woven together to form what looks to be a—chastity belt?

Seriously?

Pushing my prudishness to the side, I pull experimentally against the chains. I'm rewarded with a heavy thwack as metal snaps back on itself.

Shit! This isn't Ann Summers material. This is a real Dom toy.

But that's what he is, honey. He's a Dom. And you, little Anna, are only too willing to be his sexual toy. Admit it. You love it. The control he exerts over you. The way he takes care of you afterwards.

115

I can't deny what I already know. I love it. I love the way he looks at me like I'm something worth looking at. I love his voice in my ear, barking commands at me, pushing me onwards and upwards, awakening emotions I never even knew I possessed. I love the sensual pain of his slaps, his fingers fucking me, tongue lapping up my orgasms. Sweet Lord, I love it all. And this belt—it's just another dimension of him to explore. He asked me to trust him. I know of no better way to do that than to accept his authority and become his sub. Even if it is only for four weeks.

I flick my attention back to the metal chain before me. The links are thicker at the top, thinner at the bottom, with loops of woven metal that resemble love knots scattered throughout the links. From the waistband, four detachable chains drop, merging into a larger metal knot, about the size of a jumping jack rubber ball. And in the middle of the waist chain is a small open padlock, beautifully inscribed with my name and studded with glittering crystals.

I look guiltily around to see if Mrs. Greene has seen my gift, but as usual, she has discreetly disappeared to another part of the kitchen.

A pinging noise draws my eyes down to a phone nestled within blood-red tissue—why am I not surprised at the color? I pick it up, and I'm rewarded with a screen displaying Tyler Kane's sultry face. A message alert pings noisily beneath him.

I slide to view the message.

From: Tyler Kane
CEO Kane Enterprises
Subject: FOR YOU
Date: July 14 2016 12:01

Dear Miss Wright,
I hope you like the gift and pray I see you wearing it tonight, and every night thereafter. You are my sweet Anna, and I will never let anyone hurt you again.

Wear nothing but the belt, stockings, and high heels. Then wait for me in the billiard room. Point position, thighs parted wide, hands behind your back. Eight pm, sharp.

Tonight, little Anna, I am going to fuck that innocent little cunt of yours into submission.
xxx

Smiling giddily, I type my reply.

From: Miss Anna Wright.
Student
Subject: THANK YOU
Date: July 14 2016 12.02

Dear Mr. Kane
Looking forward to tonight, and I love the gifts.
Thank you.

Applying the belt right now.
The stockings are on standby, minus panties.

Anna xx

I smile, pocket the phone, and pick up my gifts. Then I dart up the stairs to my room. Fifteen minutes later and I'm admiring how the chain looks against my naked skin. I'm not too sure I have it on the right way, but damn, it looks sensual. And the feel of the metal knot nestled within the folds of my labia. Sweet

Lord. It's fucking hot.

I pick up the phone, pose, and post as a snap chat to Tyler with the caption, *I am so going to do myself right now.*

Several seconds later and my new phone rings. I chuckle and answer.

"Two minutes, little witch. Don't fucking move." The implication in his words is clear, but I am done being bossed about by Tyler Kane.

"And if I decide I don't want to wait for you? If I've already made plans for this afternoon?

"Oh, baby. Don't make me come looking for you."

I move forward, enjoying this new game we're playing, and yelp.

"Anna?"

"It's the belt. Tyler, it feels—ah, so good."

I rock forward onto my toes and hard cold metal slides across and up, massaging my clit deliciously. I groan wantonly.

"God damn it, Anna! You're driving me fucking insane."

I tug at the belt around my waist experimentally and bite my lip.

"Tyler." His name tumbles from my lips in a gasp of sheer pleasure.

"Open the fucking gate!" he bellows, then tires spinning and the spitting of gravel as rubber meets stone. He's at the gatehouse!

"Tell me what you're doing now." His voice is commanding and oh, so sexy.

The good girl in me flushes scarlet in innocent embarrassment, but I can't stop now. I need to stoke this fire and put it out before it consumes me. "I'm tugging the chain. Sliding it in."

"Tug it, baby. Hard. Let me hear you. Do it now."

My right hand grips and pulls hard. The metal ball at the bottom rides with bite over my throbbing sex. I moan loudly. The pain is like nothing I have ever known—it's a hungry beast gnawing deep within me, demanding to be fed. I tug the chain higher and begin to rub it backwards and forwards over my clit. "Ahhh, fuck. So. So. Good." I lose the power to converse sensibly and the phone drops to my feet forgotten as I learn how to please myself. My hips rock in tempo with my groans of delight. Lord, it feels so wrong but so, so right. I pick up speed, rubbing the metal frantically over my engorged clit in a bid to find my release. My legs tremble, and I stiffen, head thrown back in carnal delight, my heart raging within my chest.

"Tyler!" I scream as my clit spasms across the cold

metal. My legs give way, just as the door bangs open. Then Tyler Kane is on his knees, leaning over me, his mouth drinking in my cries of heated frustration.

"Tyler. Please."

I'm begging, but I don't care. I stopped caring the moment that belt entered my sex.

Sitting back on his heels he quickly unclips the belt's knotted attachments and throws them aside. His eyes lock with mine, darkest brown on green, as he unzips his fly and frees his jerking erection. "I'm going to fuck you hard, baby. You with me?"

His fingers slip into my sex and warm fluids gush to meet them. "So, fucking wet, little Anna. Wet for me?"

"Only you." I groan and rub myself shamelessly against his palm.

Tyler growls, and removing his hand he settles himself between my thighs, his hot, thick shaft knocking impatiently at the door of my virginity. I gasp and push up to meet him, but Tyler pulls back, his eyes wild with need as he fights to regain control. "Put your legs around me, baby." I do as I am told, winding my legs around his waist and moaning loudly when the head of his cock kisses my sopping sex.

"I won't lie to you, baby. My big cock in your tight little cunt is gonna hurt. You ready?"

I have never been more ready for anything in my entire life. I nod and swivel my hips to accommodate him better. He locks his lips to mine and plunges fast and deep.

Fuck! I scream against his tongue, and he laps it up, his cock buried deep.

My mouth slips from his with a slack gasp.

"Anna?" he growls, almost in desperation.

Sweet Lord. Is he asking my permission?

"Keep going. Please, Master."

Withdrawing slowly, he stalls, then eases himself back in with a steely control that steals my breath away.

I clench around him, eyes rolling back, mouth slack, incapable of even the simplest of thoughts. He repeats the process, again and again, his shirt slick with sweat, watching my every reaction with darkening eyes. Pain gives way to pleasure, and I instinctively thrust up to meet him. He hisses and stops, arms trembling, eyes wild with feral need. Fueled on by his reaction, I repeat the move and swivel my hips.

"Don't move." His tone is commanding.

I groan in frustration, while my sex clenches around Tyler's thick shaft, and milks it greedily from within.

"Fuck it. You asked for this, baby."

My heart rate spikes within me.

Grabbing my hands in one of his, Tyler yanks his belt free with the other and secures my wrists, binding them securely in thick chafing leather above my head. Then fisting my hair, he pulls hard, forcing my back to arch away from the floor. Now Tyler Kane really begins to move. Fucking me with relentless force, his cock thudding against my cervix and bruising deep.

I scream in pain and something else—pleasure. The two are inseparable and all the more arousing for it.

Tightening my thighs, I push my heels into his lower back, and am rewarded with the delicious slapping of his heavy sac against my dripping sex. I mewl in delight at the fire that's beginning to burn its way through me, awakening senses I never even knew I possessed.

"Give it to me, baby. Give." He pounds deep and grinds his pelvis in a circular motion. "It." He withdraws and repeats. "To me."

I scream high and clear. Tyler immediately claims it, crushing his mouth to mine as he jerks my body forward with the sheer power of his thrusts. My mouth goes slack, and I spasm around him as Tyler continues to fuck me without mercy.

"I missed you, Anna. Tell me!" He grunts with every

thrust of his swelling-by-the second cock. "How is that, fucking possible?"

He's still fully dressed, his fly the only thing undone.

The feeling of him on me, pinning me down, deep within me, claiming me as his own—*oh, sweet lord!*

I come again, harder than before, and still, he continues to fuck me until I can't tell where the pleasure stops and the pain begins.

I rip my hair from his fist and lift my mouth to his chest, my teeth sinking deep into his chest, tasting him in the sweat that dusts his bronzed skin and the metallic tang of his blood.

With a tortured groan, Tyler lets go, his cock jerking furiously, flooding me with his orgasm. And screaming one last time, I come with him. He spasms deep, one last deluge, his head resting against my own, his hands slack on my leather-bound wrists.

The sounds of our heavy panting fill the air. Tyler opens his eyes, and I lose any ability I ever had to breathe. He is so beautiful it hurts just to look at him.

"You okay, baby?"

I blink, tearing myself out of the trance his beauty has placed me under.

"Is it always that good?"

He shakes his head and chuckles, withdrawing

slowly and untying me. He rubs softly at my wrists then rests his head on his forearms, his dark eyes drinking me in.

"What?" I ask self-consciously.

"I like looking at you, Anna. You're like a little rabbit...only with bite." He flicks his eyes toward his chest. "And no, to answer your question, it's not always like that. Moments like that are rare. If ever."

I hear what he's saying but in a distant way. My gaze is zoned in on the blood coagulating deep within the crescent bite mark that mars the skin above his nipple.

I spring forward onto my knees, aghast at what I have done.

"Oh, my God. Tyler...I am so, so sorry."

He smiles lazily and sits up, revealing more blood-lined scratches across his skin.

I run my fingers over the marks tentatively, sick yet turned on that I could have done that to anyone.

Leaning in, he nibbles my shoulder with a grin on his beautiful lips.

"I think by this time tomorrow, you'll feel more pain than you caused me, little Yazhi."

"Yazhi?" I frown.

"I just tore through your virginity and hinted at a
125

more devilish use of that delicious body of yours, and you pick out 'Yazhi' to query me on?" He laughs incredulously and kisses me firmly.

I melt into the kiss with a soft sigh and reach down to grip him.

"Oh, no baby. We need to get you cleaned up."

I frown and follow his gaze.

"Oh no! Your carpet!" I combust with embarrassment. My blood, virtuous and red, stains the deepest, whitest carpet I have ever sunk my toes into. "I'm so sorry."

"It's of no consequence. I might even keep it like this to remind myself of my virgin conquest!" He chuckles and pulls me to my feet.

I groan at the movement and Tyler frowns. "I think I got off lightly. Shall I carry you, little Yazhi?"

I shove him away, walking stiffly and with groaning complaint toward the shower room, every muscle screaming in protest.

He scoops me up with a sigh and even washes me down, his fingers soft and oh so sensual against my oversensitive skin.

His long fingers linger on the waist chain and our eyes clash. He tugs me forward, his body hard and slick against my own. I lose all coherent thought with the first thrust of his tongue against my own. A deep rumble sounds from his chest, and placing his hands on my waist, he deftly, and with practiced ease, spins me away from him toward the shower wall.

I place my palms out against the slippery tiles and he inserts his knee between my thighs, pushing them further apart.

He soaps my breasts, palming the nipples enticingly into hard points of pink amongst the white flowing lather.

I gasp and arch back against him, feeling his erection knocking against the tight opening of my anus.

"Lesson seven, Anna. Anal."

Despite the pain that owns every square inch of me, I nod. *Oh. My. God! Tyler Kane, is going to fuck my ass.* I gulp and tense. "Will it hurt?"

"Yes." He bites my shoulder hard, and I gasp in pleasure at the pain.

"Wait here." He slaps me hard across my thighs, and the ache inside me intensifies to a pulsing hot need. How is this possible after what I just did back there in that bedroom?

Within forty seconds, he's back and purring. "We'll try this first and then when you're ready, baby, I'm going to fuck that tight little ass of yours so hard, you'll find sitting down painful."

Something long, thin, and cold buzzes into the tight opening and I gasp. Tyler grabs my throat and forces my chin up, his chest leaning across my back, holding me in place with his weight. The buzzing wand vibrates its way in slowly. I whimper in pain.

"Relax, baby. You were made for this."

The heavily lubricated wand shaft eases in, circles, then out.

I hiss and tense, not enjoying the alien sensation at all.

Tyler strokes my neck, holding me firmly in place, calming me as he eases the wand in and out. I relax, and the sensation of having a foreign object within me becomes almost pleasurable.

"You are exceptional, Anna Wright," he coos, his quickened breath fanning my ear.

This is turning him on big time! My inner voice whoops.

The wand begins to circle and a tremor of pleasure ripples through me. Moaning, I push back, but the wand is gone, replaced by the slick, thick, throbbing length of him seeking entry into that most forbidden of places.

He flexes his hips and pushes in, slowly, testing my

128

reaction. I gasp but don't pull away. "We good, baby?"

Am I? I close my eyes, and nod. I can do this.

His hands on my waist, holding me firm, Tyler inches in deeper, and a small hiss tumbles from between his clenched teeth.

Instinctively, I push against him and am rewarded with the sharp sting of his palm against my cheeks. "Don't move," he commands and repeats the process, slowly, inch by inch until his groin rests against me.

The feeling is like nothing I have ever experienced before, and if I'm honest, not one I'm enjoying. But after what he just gave me back in that room, I owe him. And if this is what turns him on, so be it.

"Circle your pelvis, Anna. Slowly."

Splaying my hands on the shower wall, I begin to swivel my hips, opening myself up to him.

"That's it, baby. Keep going." His fingers claw against my waist. Fueled on by his reaction, I repeat the action, this time with more vigor.

"Fuck!"

Another hard slap, and I stop, my breathing now just as labored as his as raw pain again gives way to pleasure.

I groan, and turning my head to the side, I see a mirror reflecting back a pale, naked woman with a bronzed Adonis buried deep within her. God, it's so erotic. I push back into him and feel his testicles slam against my sex. "Ahhh." The feeling is exquisite.

"You like it hard, don't you Anna." He flexes his hips. "Tell me."

"I love it, Master. Please..."

"You begging, Miss Wright?" His cock doesn't move.

"Yes. Please, Master. Fuck me. Fuck me hard."

"Oh baby, I intend to." His words trail off as his cock begins to sprint, my breasts slapping together with the sheer force of him. I convulse spasmodically around his pounding length, muffling a scream of pleasure against my arm.

Tyler slams deep and tilts his hips erotically. I bite off another groan of delight, the sound of wet skin slapping against wet skin turning me on even more. I watch in the mirror as he fucks me furiously, banging hard and deep. Then he stills, his body jerking as he lets go, his cum flooding me in warm jets that just keep on rolling.

The pleasure is too much. I can't take any more. I collapse into blackness with Tyler still hard, wet, and deep within me.

I WAKE TO PAIN yet again—but not where it should be. And the room, so bright earlier on is now dark, lit only with light provided by half-moon wall sconces.

I blink in confusion and lift my fingers exploratively to where the pain radiates from most.

Soft, warm, know-what-they're-doing hands grasp my fingers and pull them back to the coverlet.

"I wouldn't do that if I were you. You have quite a nasty gash there. I glued it shut, but just to be on the safe side...best not to prod it until it's had a chance to heal."

I try to push myself upright with no effect.

"Don't mean to sound ungrateful or anything, but who the hell are you?"

"My name is Dr. Stefan Rundlop. I am Tyler's friend, and his neighbor. And you, Miss Wright, are a very lucky young woman."

"And why's that?" Fuck, my head hurts.

"I was hoping you could tell me. Tyler said you fell."

I frown, trying to remember and flushing scarlet when I do. "I...I passed out," I mumble and lift the covers. Tyler's shirt covers my skin. I slump back in relief. "Where is he?" I ask, scanning the darkened room and looking for his formidable presence.

131

"I sent him downstairs for something to eat. He hasn't left your side all day." I am too tired to even try to work out why he would do that.

"What happened to my head? It hurts. A lot."

"You have a nasty concussion and a nice new scar to talk about. Your forehead and shower bracket made hard contact when you fell. As I said, you're a very lucky young woman. The force of the contact might have snapped your neck."

"Can I have something to drink, please?"

He lifts a beaker to my lips with a straw attached. "Small sips."

Common sense tells me I should listen to him, but the water is cool and I am so frigging thirsty...I drink without pausing for breath, turn to the side, and vomit.

Soft fingers ease my hair out of the flow. "I said sip, young lady." His tone is reprimanding. "You should be in the hospital, Miss Wright. If your concussion gets worse—"

I flip him away weakly as another round of retching wracks my already bruised ego. "No hospitals. Please!" I plead when the retching subsides enough to allow me to speak.

"He said you were stubborn. He wasn't wrong. Anna, if you deteriorate, we might not be able to get you to the hospital in time. Do you understand what I'm saying? You could die. Anna?"

"No hospitals," I repeat in a tone that leaves no room for argument.

He sighs wearily, like a parent giving into a very difficult child.

"It's your call. But it's against my professional advice. I'm leaving you acetaminophen. Take two, four times a day. Is your head still painful?"

"Is the Pope a Catholic?"

The good doctor laughs. Maybe he's not as dull as he seems after all.

"Maybe *this* is the best place for you after all. I see what Tyler means about you."

I snuff my disdain and wince as I push myself upright. "So, how long have you two been friends?"

"Long enough for me to know that he's infatuated with you, Miss Wright."

"I think it's the other way around." I frown at my own stupidity before adding, "You can't tell him anything we say, right? Patient confidentiality and all that."

He smiles, his eyes creasing at the corners. "Tyler's been alone for far too long, Anna. I'm glad he's finally met someone, even if that someone is his sub."

I sag back into the pillows with a soft whoomph, and close my eyes. "I'm not his sub." I sigh.

"No. You're not."

My eyes fly open. Tyler is leaning against the door fame, his face hidden in shadow. "How long have you been there?" I ask.

"Long enough. How is she Stefan?"

Stefan picks up his coat and shrugs it on. Then retrieves what I assume is his medical bag from the bottom of the bed.

"She seems alert enough, no slurred speech, pupils reactive. There was some vomiting, but that was solely due to the fact that Miss Wright refused to follow even the simplest of orders." At Tyler's scowl of confusion, the good doctor explains the incident with the water and my subsequent vomiting.

Tyler walks toward me. He looks exhausted. Not surprising, given the fact that he spent fifteen hours in the air before driving back to Wisconsin, and fucking me into oblivion. And me? I repay him by getting myself a concussion, and spending the past God knows how many hours unconscious in his bed.

"You'll keep your phone on, Stef?"

"You paying me, Ty?" Stef winks my way and grins.

"Depends on your price."

"My price is that you get some good old-fashioned shut-eye. You look like you're about ready to fall where you stand. Miss Wright, scoot over and give our boy here some room to lay down in. And Tyler, if her headache doesn't subside, or if there's any more vomiting, you phone me. Okay?"

"Vomiting, headache. Got it." Nodding wearily, he sits down on the edge of the bed and begins to pull off his socks. Then he yawns, the type of yawn that has me yawning back, and slides in next to me. "Close the door on the way out, Stef. And thanks."

"My pleasure. I'll call back tomorrow. Good night, Miss Wright."

The door closes, shutting off the light from the hallway. Tyler pulls me close and kisses my shoulder. I listen to his breathing deepen, feel the arms wrapped around me begin to slacken, and in that moment, I know— I am irrevocably in love with Tyler Kane.

ANNA

onsciousness brings with it the sun tickling my eyelids, and the sound of water splashing. Warily, I test myself in an upright position...so far so good, no head pain, no dizziness. I kick back the covers and pivot my legs around and out onto the floor. My butt and my sex scream in protest with every muscle moved. A painful reminder of virgin territory raided by none other than Tyler Kane and his territorial cock.

Cold metal slides across my waist. Reaching down I finger the links of Tyler's dominance over me. A dominance I'm stunned to admit I enjoy.

"You're awake. Good. I thought I might have to spray you with cold water to get you to open those lovely eyes of yours. How are you feeling?"

I glance up with a stupid smirk on my face.

"That good, huh?"

I drink him in like an alcoholic after Prohibition. He's dressed in Chino knee length shorts, and not much else. I gulp past the dryness in my throat as desire for him races anew through my veins.

Tyler shakes his head. "Much as I want to answer that *come fuck me* look in your eyes, I have been warned not to. Seems you're more fragile than even I anticipated."

"Your doc friend told me that *I fell*."

Tyler sits on the bed and takes my hand in his. "Something like that. It appears that I drove you into such a heated frenzy that your heart forgot to beat and your brain shut down."

"In English, please."

He sighs, entwines his fingers through my own, and frowns.

"Okay." A small smile tweaks at the corners of his mouth. "In good old English. The next time I fuck you, Miss Wright— and I assure you there will be a next time—I need to make sure you have something soft to land on." He chuckles wryly.

"God, I can't even fuck without making a damn fool of myself." Embarrassed heat floods my face.

"Hey! *I* nearly passed out! You drove me right to the very edge of my endurance and all the way back again, little witch."

He kisses my cheek and I turn toward him, seeking his lips.

He laughs and pulls back, dark eyes crinkling at the corners. God, he takes my breath away.

"Seems I have created an insatiable witch." He chuckles, slapping my thigh as he stands.

I groan in frustration and bury my face in his pillow. I want Tyler Kane inside of me, on top of me, any fucking way I can get him. Now.

"Get up baby, before I ignore the good doc's instructions and put your health in jeopardy."

Too late for that, Tyler! You did that the moment I agreed to this deal. But I can't tell him that. I can never say those words to him. So I edge towards the end of the bed instead, wincing with every movement.

"Does it hurt?" There's a wicked glint in his eyes.

I nod dolefully and push myself vertical with a hiss.

"Good! Now you'll remember where I've been and what I own every time you move."

"You're sick."

"Baby, I never pretended to be anything else."

"You might have been the first to fuck me, Tyler Kane, but that in no way means you own me. You just hired me."

138

Slowly, very slowly...God, it hurts...I raise my hands and twist my hair up into a loose chignon. The movement forces my breasts up and forwards. I smile as Tyler's breath hitches, and watching him carefully, I push my elbows further back. A small muscle jumps along the side of his jaw.

I smile victoriously and lowering my hands, I slide them across the silver belt around my waist, my eyes travelling down his flat stomach to the prominent V that dips beneath his waistband.

Tyler's eyes immediately darken and primal hunger emanates from him like honey from a beehive.

"Careful, baby. I might take that statement as a challenge and ensure you never want anyone but me."

Oh, Tyler, I'm already there. I limp past him, my body pale and bruised. Who knew sex could be so hazardous to one's health, yet so fucking good at the same time?

With deliberation in my every movement, I brush past him, grazing a pert nipple across his left arm as I pass.

He stiffens, his jaw clenching, eyes narrowed.

"Honey..." I smile. "That works both ways!"

Walking into the bathroom, I leave behind a

stunned—and horny if the bulge in his shorts is anything to go by—Tyler Kane.

Round two to me. *Go, Anna*! My inner voice whoops, but it's a hollow victory considering I'm already dreading leaving him when my time's up.

With pain in my every movement, I dismiss a shower in favor of a relaxing bath. I think I've earned one.

I lower myself onto the edge of a bath sunk into cold black granite, and groan.

Tyler watches from the doorway with an amused glint in his eyes.

"Shall I help you, little witch?"

"Depends."

"On what?"

He walks forward, rolling up his sleeves with every step.

"On what you want in return?"

He unscrews a bottle of honey-colored liquid and pours it under the running water. Jasmine instantly perfumes the rising steam, filling the bathroom with its sensual aroma.

"I want what I have always wanted, Anna. Your complete trust, and your total submission."

"Keep dreaming. Haven't you got somewhere else to be?"

"Anna, I have at least a dozen places I should be, but only one I want to be."

My heart lurches to a stop. How can he say things like that and not expect me to fall in love with him? I try to restart my heart with flippancy. "Careful Mr. Kane, a comment like that could get you laid."

He shakes his head and chuckles. "Much as I would like to get laid right now, Miss Wright, I'm afraid I would have to decline such an offer. I have a conference call at ten."

"Don't let me keep you then."

He ignores me and places a pile of fluffy white towels on a bench to my left.

"Seriously, I can manage here. Go already."

"As your Dom, I have a duty to look after you, Anna, just as your duty is in pleasing me."

"You're going to watch me bathe?" I ask incredulously. Are there no boundaries this man won't cross to get what he wants?

Leaning across me and extending his bronzed arm, he opens the taps. The water instantly begins to boil and bubble as the bath's air jets kick in.

Leaning forward, he kisses my nose and grins. "Watch? No, Anna. I'm going to bathe you, and we can talk as I do."

141

"I'm not a baby, Tyler. I can do it myself!"

"It's not open to discussion. Now get in the tub and lie back."

He turns the water off but leaves the jets on.

I open my mouth to argue, and he cocks that damn eyebrow again. The last time he did that, my butt took a hiding from his overly enthusiastic hand. And the way my ass feels after yesterday...

I climb in and lean back with a small groan. Hell, I ache all over. Inside and out.

"Good girl."

Grabbing a sponge, he lathers it up and begins to wash me, neck to toes clean. I must admit, it's not half as bad as I thought it was going to be.

He discards the sponge and dips a hand beneath the bubbles, his palm drifting across a nipple. I arch into his touch, a soft gasp of pleasure falling from my lips.

"So responsive, little Yazhi." He smiles and keeps up the slow torture with his hand.

I lick my lips and close my eyes.

"I own you, do I not, little Anna?"

I nod my head. "Yes."

"Yes, what, baby?"

"Yes. Yes, Master."

I mewl wantonly as the fingers of his other hand slip

between the folds of my sex and circle with intoxicating slowness.

I gasp and open my thighs to him.

His fingers pull hard at a nipple, clamping the pert bud between thumb and finger. Squeezing hard at the precise second, he thrusts a finger inside me, fanning my clit with his nail.

"Ahhh!" I lift my head back above water, and Tyler tugs my nipple painfully higher.

"Look at me, Anna."

I snap open my eyes, and green eyes meet blazing brown.

One finger becomes two, pistoning in and out, his thumb locked on my clit, torturing me with slow sensual strokes.

"Shall I make you come like this, Anna? Tell me."

"Yes!"

"Yes, what, baby?" Three fingers now, fucking me hard and fast.

"Yes! Master, please!"

"Please, what?"

Too late. I coil around him, gasping as my release builds.

Tyler chuckles. "Oh, no, Anna. Not yet. I have a conference call to prepare for and you, baby, will not touch yourself in any way until I get back. If you do, I will punish you. Now. Relax."

He's ending his domineering session? What? No! Not yet!

Towel drying his hands, he walks into the bedroom, leaving me with a raging fire deep inside of me and a gaping mouth.

"What the fuck!"

"I heard that, baby," he calls from the bedroom.

Childishly, I throw the sponge after him.

ANNA

For the next three days, Tyler Kane attends to my every need, but one. After his conference call, he took me to lunch, introduced me to his collection of classic cars, and gave me my first ever ride on the back of a motorbike—a shining hulk of metal with Ducati stenciled across its tank in block silver. But not once did he finish what he started in that bath. I tried everything, but he was resolute in his denial of me. He would not touch me, he stated calmly, until the good doctor Stefan declared me *fully fit to fuck.* His words not mine.

By the time Stefan finally gets around to giving me a clean bill of health, three whole days and nights have passed, and I am a ticking time bomb of hormonal need, ready to explode at even the slightest touch.

Tyler is in a meeting in his study when my phone buzzes.

I look at the screen and my heart lurches.

From: Tyler Kane

CEO Kane Enterprises

Subject: PLAY TIME

Date: July 18 2016 14:21

Dear Miss Wright,

I have an itch that needs scratching. Think you could help me out?

Xxx

My inner sub falls to her knees, lowers her head and spreads her thighs wide.

And me? I text my reply with shaking fingers and a stupid smile splayed across my face.

From: Anna Wright

Student

Subject: ITCH

Date: July 18 2016 14:23

Dear Mr. Kane,

I am afraid, due to the unknown cause of your itch, that I will have to decline until further investigations are carried out.

Xxx

From: Tyler Kane

CEO Kane Enterprises

Subject: Duly noted

Date: July 18 2016 14:24

Dear Miss Wright,

Contagion will not be a problem, however, I cannot rule out the risk of explosion, and request your immediate presence in my study to investigate this matter further.

From: Anna Wright

Student

Subject: Explosion

Date: July 18 2016 14:25

Dear Mr. Kane,

Please, do not touch the affected area. I am on my way.

I can't wipe the stupid grin from my face as I run

past Mrs. Greene and down the staircase toward Tyler Kane's study.

I knock nervously on his door, and wipe my palms across the full knee-length skirt Tyler had laid out for me to dress in this morning, along with a poplin-sleeved shirt, suspenders, stockings, a delicate little lacy bra, and matching G-string.

The door opens and Tyler invites me inside with a salacious smile and an erection that threatens to explode the stitching of his fly.

"That's your itch?"

"Part of it." He silences me with a raised finger circling in the air, and removes his clothes. After a second's hesitation, I fulfil his silent command, and strip, my clothes pooling in a small pile at my feet. I step free of the material with a question falling from my tongue moistened lips. "And the other part?"

"Come." He extends his hand toward me in invitation.

I place my hand in his and allow him to lead me toward a sturdy book case in the corner of the room.

With a soft nudge of his hand, the whole thing, books and all, swings inwards.

Trying unsuccessfully to calm my thudding heart, I

follow Tyler through the opening into a room unlike anything I have ever seen. The book case closes behind us.

Tyler lets go of my hand and walks over to a large stereo system complete with killer speakers, and begins to punch buttons. One of my all-time favorite songs instantly booms around the room—Awolnation, "Sail." The dark tension that exists between us in this strange room instantly heightens.

I look at Tyler. He looks back, his face impassive, controlled, dark with things I have no experience of.

"What is this place, Tyler?"

"A play room."

"Not your dungeon?"

"No. You are not ready for that type of pain yet."

"So this is what turns you on? Pain?"

"Pain, your complete trust in me, your total submission."

"And if I say no?"

"You are free to leave any time you wish, Anna."

"And our arrangement?"

"Will continue as before. This, however, is what turns me on, Anna. I never pretended otherwise."

"But all this—" I stretch out my arm and sweep it around, trying to encompass the enormity of what this room represents, and failing miserably.

"Is an extension of what we have done already. Do you trust me, Anna?"

"You know I do."

"Then show me."

"How?"

"Point."

His voice commands my total obedience and I immediately fall to my knees at his feet. For several minutes I stay in my submissive crouch, head bent, eyes averted, heart thudding like a jack hammer in my chest and ears.

"Anna, look at me."

I lift my head. Tyler is standing before me, glorious in his nakedness and holding a set of wide, leather cuffs complete with heavy metal carabiner attachments. I gulp back my fear and hold his gaze.

"I am going to cuff you with these, Anna. They are called spacer cuffs. They will distribute your weight, and if I so desire it, they will keep you open to me. I will suspend you horizontally, face forward, from the spacer bar hanging above us. Nod if you are with me, Anna."

I nod, feeling more nervous than I have ever felt

during one of his scenes, but desperate for more. "Yes, Master."

"Good girl. Now stand up and lift your hands out in front of you."

I obey him without further question, and he attaches the heavy-duty cuffs to my wrists and secures them tightly. My breathing accelerates.

"What are you going to do to me, Master?"

"Do not speak, Anna. Screaming, panting, groaning is allowed and, if I feel inclined and you please me, I may let you beg. But not unless I give permission. Nod if you're okay with this, Anna. If not, I will unshackle you right now, and you can go back to your room."

Do I want this? This is some seriously messed up shit. But God, I am so turned on by it. I nod, head down as instructed.

"Good girl. You may look at me, Anna."

I lift my gaze, and the fire within me flares with desire.

Tyler Kane naked is a glorious sight to behold, his body glistening with vitality, his erection bobbing high and proud before him. In his hands, he's holding two separate chain clamps with end attachments.

"These are nipple clamps, Anna. I am going to attach them to those pert little rosettes of yours. If you're good with this, Anna, nod yes."

I nod, hissing as the clamps are attached and pleasure and pain kick in.

Tyler stands back and smiles. Then turning quickly on his heel, he walks over to the well-stocked wall rack. From this, he takes another set of cuffs with large carabiner attachments, and a leather flogger that has a silver, curved ball-end handle.

Dipping down, he attaches the cuffs to my ankles, then stands. "I am going to lower the spacer bar, Anna. As it lowers, you will bend and grip your ankles. I want you to stay in that position until I attach your cuffs, to the spacer bar. When I am happy you are secure, I will raise the bar. Nod if you are good with being suspended, Anna."

I shake my head. Tying up is one thing, hanging me from a fucking metal bar attached to the ceiling? Not good, not good at all.

"Anna, I would never do anything that would put you in danger. Trust me, baby." He steps closer. Cupping my sex within his palm he inserts three fingers. And with lazy slowness, he begins finger fucking me until I'm panting with unsated need.

152

Sweet Lord, what this man can do with his fingers should be outlawed.

"Trust me, baby. Let me do this."

I concede with a groan of unadulterated pleasure, and Tyler kisses me hard, his tongue twisting around my own, owning it. Owning me.

"You are an amazing woman, Anna Wright. My woman. All mine." Removing his fingers, he steps back and pulls the thick metal bar above me down to waist level.

"I'm going to attach your wrist cuffs to these short chains, Anna. Your ankles I will attach to the longer chains. Then I will hoist you up with this." He shows me a small remote, no different from a car key fob. "You good with this, baby?"

Fuck no! My inner self screams frantically. But outer me is looking into Tyler Kane's dark, dark eyes and salivating at what that look promises.

"Yes, Master."

"Thank you, Anna. Your trust means a lot to me."

He attaches my bound wrists to the shorter chains, then pulls the bar down slowly, forcing me to bend until my hands meet my ankles. Grabbing my ankle cuffs, he clips them to the bar with the heavy carabiners, and stands back with a lazy grin. Then a slight buzzing. His hands support me cradle style, and Anna Wright is airborne, legs and arms spread, face up. I have never in my life felt as exposed or vulnerable.

"Oh, baby. I like you like this. I like it a lot." He flicks his hand and the whip I saw him lift down from the rack trails across my sex in a swift kiss of pain.

I arch against the chains that bind me, and hiss.

"We good, baby?"

"Yes, Master."

He whips me again, but instead of the pain I had expected, a delectable wave of hedonism ripples through me taking me close to that beautiful point of release.

"More, Anna?"

"More, Master. Please."

"Look at me."

I flick my gaze to where he stands between my legs. The whip has been flipped so that the silver ball handle faces me. "I am going to fuck you with this, slowly at first and then hard. Are you good with this, Anna?"

I look at his erection, thick, full, and jerking hungrily. There is no choice. There never was.

"Yes. Thank you, Master."

He grins a feral smile and slides the ball end of the

handle into his mouth. He winds his tongue around the silver and sucks before pulling it free and inserting it slowly, into my sex. Then he stops.

"Tell me, Anna. Tell me what you want," he breathes.

"More. I want more. Please, Master." I'm begging, but I don't care. I stopped caring the second he inserted that cold, hard metal within me.

He plunges deeper, out, in, over and over, picking up momentum as his own desire flares. The chains above me rattle, keeping time with his impetus. I am so close. So fucki—

"Yes, baby. Yes. Give it to me!"

Gasping, I let go, arching high, my screams of pleasure drowning out his encouraging voice. Then he's in me, pistoning in and out like a fucking steam train on Viagra. His grunts of pleasure fueling me on to higher heights. *Sweet Lord.* My heart stutters. Stops. Kicks in again. Tyler yells my name and thrusts deep, his orgasm exploding within me, taking me over the edge of pleasure with him.

I close my eyes and relax into my hammock of leather and chains, willing my hammering heart to slow down. Tyler rests across me, his lips claiming mine while his heart thrums against my own.

"Baby, you are exquisite."

"Hmmm…"

He chuckles and removes himself from between my legs. "Let's get you down. Legs first." He unshackles my ankles and rubs each leg briskly before setting them on the floor.

"Mmm." His eyes twinkle mischievously. "I like you like this, Anna. I like it a lot. Hands all trussed up like that, nipples clamped. Mmmm mmm."

I wrestle against my chains. He can't be serious. Not after all that. My eyes flick to his cock. It's thick, hard, and elongating by the second. "Fuck!"

"Oh, baby, I intend to."

He walks back to his toy corner and returns wearing a strap-on just as big as his own erect cock. His fist glides up and down its length coating it wetly with lubricant.

I gulp and try to pull myself free of the chains that still bind my wrists.

"Tyler. No."

"No?" He slides a soft hand across my throat and circles to stand behind me.

"You heard me. I said no."

He nips my shoulder and cups my sex, teasing it

156

with butterfly strokes that have me panting with need all over again.

I arch into him, the chains above us rattling as my frustration grows.

"More Anna?"

"Yes, Master. Please."

His fingers cup my breast, clawing deep and I gasp.

"You were born for this, baby. Born to please me. Let me please you, Anna."

I moan and push back against him, needing more.

"Yes. Yes. Anything. Please, Master. Please."

Walking around to stand in front of me, he grips my thighs, lifts them high and secures them around his waist. His hands circle my hips tightly. "Oh, baby, I'm going to make you scream."

With a grunt of undiluted power, he rams deep.

I scream loud and clear. Oh, my sweet lord! The sensation of having him fill me so entirely is electrifying. I quiver around him, dangerously close to letting go.

Tyler slaps me warningly, once, twice, three times in quick succession. His breathing is harsh with excitement as he yanks me back and pushes me forward, sliding me on and off his cock, and strap-on, with a speed that leaves me gasping for air.

I tremble as the pressure within me mounts, and Tyler slaps me hard again, dulling the fire and denying me my release.

"Tell me you don't fucking love this. Tell me!"

"I love it, all of it!" I tighten my thighs, using the leverage the chains give me to circle his pounding cock and strap-on. He groans, his fingers digging into my hips.

The added pain is all I need to push me over, and I scream his name as I come, my orgasm a tsunami of pleasure that steals my breath away.

"Yes, baby, give it to me!" He rams deep then stills, his cock jerking stream after stream of hot semen deep within me until there is nothing left to give and he folds on top of me.

"Relax. Fuck, Anna. When will I ever get enough of you?"

I roll my shoulders and groan. I don't want to think about time frames. Not here. Not now. It's bad enough that I love him without crumbling in front of him as well. I sniff back a tear and slide my legs free of his relaxed grip.

He pulls out and steps in front of me. The strap-on has been removed, and he's frowning. "Anna, if I was hurting you that much, you should have called *'Black'*."

"No. It isn't you. It's the chains. I can't feel my hands." It's lame, but it's all I've got.

He nods and releases me from the cuffs, rubbing my chafed skin and kissing my wrists.

This is the man I love. This gentle, thoughtful person who cares that my wrists hurt and kisses them. "Better?" His voice is as tender as his hands are.

"Much better."

"Can you walk?"

I don't know. Can I? I step forward, and my leg buckles beneath me.

Tyler's arms are around me in an instant, lifting me up and cradling me against his chest.

"I can walk. Just give me a second." I push against his arms, but he only tightens them.

"I'm your Master, Anna. I have a duty of care. Carrying you when you need me to is just one of those obligations. I had Mrs. Greene make up the bed for us. We can rest there."

He carries me into a room just as opulent as the play room is stark, and lays me down on a bed soft with pale blue silk.

"Lie on your tummy baby. I need to take care of

159

those slap marks I left you with."

I do as I am told and am rewarded with his warm hands massaging aromatic oil into my skin. "I'm afraid I went overboard with the slapping. You have two large bruises in the shape of my hands on your delectable butt, Miss Wright."

"I thought that would make you happy," I snipe.

"I am not a monster, Anna. Bruising you brings me no pleasure."

"But causing me pain does." It's not a question.

"Yes, it does."

I flip around to face him, and he covers me with a soft throw that matches the blue of the silk I lie on.

"Why?"

"You could ask yourself the same question, Anna. When you bit my chest that time, it turned you on, did it not?"

I frown, trying to dismiss what he's saying as rubbish, but I can't. I'm just as bad as he is, maybe even more so because I like the pain he inflicts on me. I like it a lot.

He sighs and slips beneath the throw to face me, his dark eyes searching as he waits for my reply.

"That's not a fair analogy."

"I think it is. When you're exploding around my

cock, screaming my name, remember it's the pain that's helped get you there. You love it, Anna. Whether you admit it to yourself or not, you love it."

He's right, but I am damned if I'm going admit it. Not to him. Not to anyone. I change the subject quickly. "How many have you brought here, Tyler?"

"You really want me to answer that one? Seriously?"

I lick my lips and nod.

"In this room right here, or any of the other rooms in my house—none. Into the room next door, too many to count with accuracy."

"Were they your girlfriends?"

Pain slices through my chest. Why am I doing this to myself?

"No. Until you, I never felt it necessary to engage in useless chitchat. They were subs who needed a Master, and after a vigorous health screening, I obliged. I fucked them. Nothing more, nothing less."

"What about Lilith?" I throw at him.

"Lilith is a trainee sub in the lifestyle. She is also Mrs. Greene's niece and off limits. She would have my balls on a plate if I so much as even looked in her niece's direction. Not that I ever would. She's not my type."

"And I am?"

"Yes. Big hips, small waist, full, natural breasts, and let's not get started on that mighty fine ass of yours."

"That's not what I meant."

"What do you want me to say, Anna? That I like spending time with you? That I like waking up with you in my bed? Or listening to you laugh? That I've never felt like this before? Not with anyone. That it scares me shitless. You really want to hear that, baby? 'Cause, honestly, I don't."

Tyler drops his eyes and nuzzles the skin on his arm. When he looks at me again, his eyes are hooded.

"Your turn. Honesty at all times. Remember. Why were you crying back there?"

"I'm scared."

"Of me?"

"Of what's going to happen next." At least that part's true.

"Baby, you know what's going to happen next. The same thing that always happens whenever you're near me. My cock buried deep in that greedy little cunt of yours. Fucking it hard."

"Could you be any crasser?"

"At least I'm calling it as it is."

"And I'm not?"

"No. You're not. This is a business deal made between two consenting adults, Anna. You wanted money and training. The money you have, the training I'm working on and unapologetically enjoying every damn minute of it. What else do you want?"

I roll away from him. I don't want to see the pity in his eyes when he figures it out.

With an exasperated sigh, he spoons around me, folding me into his embrace, his heartbeat strong and steady against my back. Just like I'm going to have to be to survive the experience of ever having known Tyler Kane.

WHEN I WAKE IN the morning, it's to Tyler Kane watching me with dark eyes and a sweet smile on his beautiful face. My heart flares to life within my chest. God, how will I live without him when the time comes? Sadness overwhelms me and with great difficulty, I gulp it down.

"Hey, Yazhi."

He rolls above me, his maleness nestling against my sex.

"What does it mean?" I whisper.

He arches an eyebrow. "What? Yazhi?"

I nod, eyes drinking him in, committing him to memory.

163

"Little one. It means 'little one.' It is an affectionate term given to someone you care for in my native language."

"Native?"

"I'm Navajo, Anna."

He kisses my nose and flexing his hips, slides his thick shaft deep within me.

I wrap myself around him and forget whatever it was I had been about to say.

OVER THE FOLLOWING WEEKS, when he isn't working, Tyler Kane makes me forget everything but him, fucking me into submission in every way possible, in every room, with every implement at his disposal. I now know every sexual term and toy intimately. From fisting to lemon pie and everything between the two. My body aches in places I didn't know existed. I have bruises fading into bruises and a slight burning when I pee. I mention it to Tyler, and he laughs.

"Cystitis, Anna. It's also known as the honeymooner's disease."

"Oh."

He pushes his paperwork aside and pulls me onto his lap.

"Yes. 'Oh'." He kisses me warmly, his eyes alight with mischief. "I thought since this was your last day, we could go out for a drive?"

"Are you asking me, Master Kane?"

"Yes, Miss Wright, I believe I am. Plus we've exhausted every room here so—"

I slap his shoulder and stand up. How easy it is to be with him now that I know everything there is to know about him. I smile and force the pain down that threatens to engulf me at the thought of leaving him.

"Out sounds good."

He looks at me quizzically but lets the tremor in my voice go without comment.

I leave him to his paperwork, rushing from the room before he can witness the tears already beginning to slip from my eyes.

TYLER

Anna sat beside him in his convertible Porsche, all big green eyes and infectious happiness.

He smiled, feeling happier than he had in a long time, and slipped the car into first. It purred forward with ease. He pushed the gearbox into second, third, fourth, and almost a million dollars' worth of Italian engineering streaked down the drive toward the main road with ease.

The gates were already opened. Daniel and his brother must have heard him coming. Daniel tipped his forelock respectfully while his younger brother winked cheekily at Anna.

Jealousy flared to life within him. He was tempted to slam the brakes on and fire the boy on the spot. Instead, he glanced at Anna, trying to gauge her mood. Damn, but she was beautiful, her auburn hair whipping about her face, lips parted, perfect white teeth on show for all to see as she laughed like a truanting school girl.

"Smiling at the hired help can be a dangerous pastime, baby."

"Ditto, Mr. Kane," she threw back with a smile. "And just for the record, I only have eyes for you and that lovely gear stick you're fondling so expertly."

He laughed loud and free, and acting on nothing more than good old impulse, he leaned in and kissed her hard and quick.

"So where are we going, stud?" She grinned.

"Anna, so help me! I'm trying to be a gentleman, and you're not helping."

"Okay, okay, I'll behave…for now."

He laughed at the mischief in her voice. God, she was a delight to be around.

The scenery picked up speed, sliding by in a blur of greens and shimmering blue. At his side, Anna sat with hands raised high and grinning like a child set loose in a wind tunnel.

Looking at her like this, her long hair whipping in the wind, her green eyes sparkling…she was everything he wanted and more. So, much more. He grinned and shook his head as the road dipped lower, taking them ever closer to a small harbor complete with a bobbing yacht—his yacht.

"You're taking me out on a boat?" She whooped.

He smiled and flicked her a teasing look. "Something like that."

"You're not going to tell me, are you?" She pouted, and his cock jerked at the thought of those lips around— *Stop it!*

He shifted in his seat and tore his gaze away from her mouth. "I thought we could spend the day snorkeling."

"Like flippers and stuff?"

"I take it by the *stuff* statement you haven't snorkeled before, Miss Wright."

She shook her head and closed her eyes, face pointed toward the sun. "The river Clyde's too cold to snorkel in, Mr. Kane."

He frowned, and easing the car into his reserved spot within the marina's bay, he killed the engine. "I wasn't talking about the Clyde, Anna. Surely you have holidayed?"

She scowled and shook her head. "This is the first time I have been anywhere outside of Glasgow. Like I keep telling you, Tyler, me and you, we come from different worlds."

Images of her scars drifted like tumbleweeds into

168

his mind. He shut them down quickly, climbed from the car, and forced a smile onto his face. "Not anymore, Anna, not with the money you have in that little bank account of yours. Come. Let me show you how I like to spend my money."

He opened her door, and taking her hand in his, he guided her toward the marina's dock and his baby—a ninety-foot yacht named Silver.

Anna walked silently beside him, a vision of beauty in a cute little A-line sundress and matching lace pumps. She had complained about not having jeans to throw on, but jeans were not the chosen attire for his subs—too fucking inaccessible. This way she looked beautiful and he got easy access. His cock twitched hungrily again. What the fuck was it with this girl and his cock? He had lost all control over his most prized possession the moment he had laid eyes on her. Another first and not one he was enjoying, not in public anyway.

Shoving his hand into his shorts, he pinched his shaft warningly, and it deflated back to a less noticeable size.

"Where are we?" Her eyes flitted around, drinking in the lake, the scattered condos, the bobbing boats.

"Sister Bay. And that big boat over there—" He directed her gaze toward *Silver,* growling her way into the docking station with his employee, friend, and fellow life-styler, Mara, at her wheel. "This is where we're going to be spending the day. Tonight, I thought we could spend in my condo. If you're agreeable, that is?"

She stopped and looked up at him, an amused tilt to her mouth. "If I'm agreeable? You sure you're okay, Tyler?"

"Baby, I have never been better. Now, shall we?"

She chuckled and shook her head as Mara threw down a mooring rope for him to catch. He caught it deftly, wrapped and knotted it, and smiled up at Mara.

"Hey, Tyler. Good to see you back. You checking on your interests or just having a day off?" she asked, jumping the last few feet between herself and the dock with practiced ease.

"A bit of both, Mara. This is my friend, Anna. Anna," he smiled, "this is Mara, my dock master."

Mara stuck her hand out with a quick questioning look at Tyler, and Anna clasped it politely, a shy smile tugging at her mouth.

"Hi, Anna. Welcome to Sister Bay. I've left your gear in the master bedroom along with Tyler's. Tyler, there's a picnic basket in the kitchen, and the other stuff, it's in a black hold-all in your wardrobe."

"Thanks, Mara."

"You're welcome. Shall I arrange to have your dinner delivered or will you be dining at the Waterfront?"

"I don't know. Anna? What would you prefer?"

She shrugged. "I'm great either way."

"Oh! Your accent! You from Scotland, Anna?"

"For my sins. This place is stunning."

"You should have seen it before Tyler bought it over. It was a real eyesore. Now—well, you can see for yourself."

Fuck! He was so going to kill Mara.

"You own this place?"

"Oh, honey, he doesn't just own the marina. Tyler owns everything within a fifteen-mile radius of here. You playing pauper to impress the girl, Tyler?"

"You would know all about playing, Mara."

"Touché. Now, reservation or not?"

Memories of the last time they had visited a restaurant together flitted across his mind, along with the flirtatious waiter she had made him apologize to. He shook his head firmly. "Have the chef cook brie ravioli for Anna and a shrimp risotto for myself. Say, seven? In my chalet, and can you be here to lock down Silver

171

for me?"

"I can't, but I'll make sure Bert is here to take care of her for you."

"You got a date lined up?" He cocked an eyebrow inquisitively.

"Seriously, Ty, Rina would whip me with shell ends if she so much as thought, for even one tiny little second, that I was tailing it both ends. You better than anyone should know how she is."

Anna looked between himself and Mara quizzically, and he felt obliged to explain. "Mara is in the lifestyle, Anna. Her girlfriend Rina is a high-ranking Mistress. It was Rina who introduced me to the lifestyle."

"Oh!" Her mouth popped open, and her green eyes widened in shock.

Mara chuckled. "We were all newbies once, Anna. Don't worry. Before you know it, you'll be whipping his balls. Nice meeting you, honey, and if you need to vent, Tyler has my number on speed dial. Tyler, you be good to her, ya hear?"

He flicked his forelock. "Yes, ma'am."

She dropped the keys into his palm and disappeared quickly in the opposite direction.

"You fucked her too, Tyler?"

Seriously. They were going to do this in the middle

of the fucking marina? He grabbed her hand and yanked her up the gangplank behind him.

"Like I said, Rina and Mara introduced me to the BDSM scene. Rina runs the local club and sex shop. Thanks to her, I have a bag of goodies on board to try out with you if you're agreeable?"

She pulled her hand from his, fists balled at her side.

"Answer the damned question, Tyler. Did you sleep with Mara?"

Fuck it. Anna wanted the truth…he'd give it to her. "Slept? No. Fucked in every way possible? Yes. But only in a club setting. Never in my house and never in my boat."

"So, what? I'm supposed to feel honored now? Seriously!"

He stepped onto the deck and yanked her behind him, his anger mounting with every syllable falling from her damned perfect little mouth.

"I had a life before you, baby! Accept it and move on! Now, if you'll excuse me, I have a boat to start." He dropped her hand and strode quickly towards the control room before he said something he'd regret later on.

What the fuck was her damned problem anyway? Any other sub would have been jumping for joy if he'd taken them on a trip like this. *But she's not your sub, is she, Ty? Her opinions matter to you.*

"Fuck off," he hissed into empty air and rammed the accelerator forward. Engines grumbled in complaint, and Tyler eased off with a scowl.

"You really want me to? Just say the word, and I'm outta here."

He frowned down at the controls and began punching in the coordinates. That done, he hit Auto on the EV-100.

"I wasn't talking to you," he grumbled.

"So I noticed."

He spun around, anger purring and ready for release. And then he froze. *Fuck!* In the time it had taken him to start the boat and ease out of the harbor, she had stripped down to her bikini and was sitting in the plush corner suite with nothing but two black scraps of material to cover her. The chastity chain he had gifted her with, glistened along her small waist before dipping beneath her bikini bottoms enticingly.

His cock sprung to attention, slapping against his naval with a wet *thwap.*

"You like?" she purred.

Damn Anna Wright to hell and back! She took his control and spat it in his face. But not today. No! Today he was taking control back. His sac tightened in complaint, and with a low hiss, he turned back to his controls.

"Go put something more appropriate on until we're out of the bay. After that, you can do as you wish."

Are you insane! his inner voice screamed in sympathy with his erection. But before Tyler could change his mind, the door to the cabin clicked shut, and Anna was gone.

Pre-cum soaked his shorts, making him even more fucking frustrated. Shit! Spinning on his heel, Tyler headed for the bathroom located in the saloon next to the master suite. He needed a cold shower pronto if he was going to make it through the rest of the day without gagging her little mouth and fucking her into submission.

Anna was curled up, still in her bikini, trying to figure out how to work the TV controls. His cock twitched towards her. He ignored it and marched into the bathroom where he slipped off his shorts and kicked them away. He slapped the shower on and stepped beneath the warm spray. He needed release before he caved completely and gave her what she so fucking obviously wanted—his cock on a platter.

Lathering his hands, he quickly fisted his erection

and began pumping the thick shaft, slowly at first, and then as his desire mounted, with impetus. The door slid open, and Anna walked in, her eyes falling to his pumping fist and hunched shoulders.

And then she was at him, her lips against his back, hands wrapping around his cock and mirroring his fisting action. He should tell her to fuck off but he was too far gone.

"Point! On your knees!" he hissed. Instantly, and to his surprise and confusion, she fell to her knees before him.

"Place your hands on my thighs and open your mouth. Ahhh! Fuck!" She was already on him, licking and sucking, her eyes on his. Tyler rolled back his head and groaned as Anna nipped the silky head of his cock, dipping the tip of her tongue into the small opening and lapping up his pre-cum. He moaned in abject pleasure, and she sucked deeper, harder. Her lips clamped against his shaft, working it zealously. He bucked into her, holding her head tight against him as he fucked her smart mouth silent.

"Yes! Fuuuck!" He thrust deep, his orgasm spurting in hot, thick streams down her throat, and Anna swallowed it all without one gag in sight. Sweet Lord, what was that girl made of?

He pulled her to her feet and kissed her deeply, savoring the taste of himself within her mouth. She pushed herself against him, but he still had control, and he wasn't willing to let it go just yet. Anna Wright needed to learn her place.

"I'm going to fuck you, Anna. But not here," he whispered against her mouth. "There's a billiard table next to the room you were just in. I want you to go there and lie on the table face down, hand and legs splayed towards the pockets. Go!"

"Yes, Master." She nodded, trotting off and leaving a trail of water in her wake.

God, she was exquisite, and after only four weeks. What would she be like after a few months? *You don't have a few months, Ty. She goes home tomorrow.* "We'll fucking see about that," he answered himself. And slapping the water off, he marched into the adjoining bedroom and slipped on a dry pair of shorts. From the black bag in his wardrobe, he pulled out a mouth gag and a set of under-bed ties.

Time to introduce little Anna Wright to the gag.

She was lying as he had instructed, minus her bikini. That in itself was a punishment. He hadn't told her to take it off. But she was still learning, and she had pleased him in the shower.

Anna turned her head to look at him, and Tyler slapped her thighs hard. She squeaked and turned her face away.

"Good girl. Anna, I am going to tie you to the legs of the table. Are you with me, baby?"

"Yes."

Her voice was a husky rasp that yanked at his dick enticingly.

"That pleases me, Anna. It pleases me very much that you trust me so much."

"I trust you, Master. Only you."

It took all of his restraint not to abandon the scene and make love to her like she deserved. But if he did that, he gave it all up. Years of control gone in the blink of one of her lovely green eyes. He wasn't strong enough for that yet. Not even for her.

He picked up the gag and unbuckled it. "I'm going to gag you, baby. I don't want anyone hearing your screams but me. Open your mouth."

"What are you going to do to me, Master?"

He tugged the straps into place and began the process of binding her wrists and ankles to the chain tethers.

Then he slapped her ass, harder than before. She moaned into the cloth but didn't question him again.

"Shhh, baby. Open your mouth." Obediently, she opened her mouth, eyes hidden under the curtain of auburn hair falling across her face and over her pale shoulders. He removed his shorts, climbed up onto the table, and silenced her smart mouth with the ball gag.

"Oh, baby, I have wanted to tame you like this since the first time you opened that fucking smart mouth of yours." He trailed a finger down her back, through the valley of her mighty fine ass and into her sex. Jesus! She was so fucking wet. With a small grunt, he stretched the spiked cock ring over his erection, groaning as the rubber snapped into place, thickening his shaft instantly. Then he stretched himself over her, flexed his hips forcefully, and thrust deep and without mercy.

She screamed into the gag.

"I own this baby, every orgasm, every gasp, every fucking scream, belongs to me. Just, me." He began to move, fucking her harder than he ever had before, his cock slamming deep, over and over, again and again, until she anointed his pounding shaft with her orgasm. And still it wasn't enough. He wanted more. Pushing his groin against her, he gyrated his hips, relishing the feel of her tightening around him, squeezing his cock. *God!* The feeling was exquisite, and not one he relished giving up anytime soon.

Gripping her shoulders, he arched her back against his chest, fueling himself on with the glorious sight of her breasts while he fucked her.

"So good, baby." He gripped a mound and squeezed firmly.

This time, she bucked back to meet him, matching his rhythm, thrust for perfect thrust until finally, she orgasmed yet again, her engorged clitoris chafing against his cock.

"Fuck! Anna." He bucked deep and stayed there, emptying himself into her in spasmodic jerks that stole all reasoning and left him breathless.

For several minutes, he lay spent on top of her, panting himself back to earth. Jesus. How could he give this up? Give Anna Wright up?

He couldn't. Not now. Not ever. He needed Anna Wright, and the realization galled him.

Feeling now back in his legs and arms, he slipped his hard, wet cock from her sopping sex and eased it into her mighty fine ass.

She screamed, pulling against the restraints. He stopped, giving her time to get used to the feeling of his cock buried deep in that glorious little orifice, and

180

sliding his hand beneath her stomach, Tyler pulled her butt higher, relishing the pleasure the movement created. Anna moaned beneath him, and he gave up all restraint, fucking her with a ferocity that shocked even himself until at last he orgasmed, and collapsed spent upon her sweat-slickened back.

When his breathing returned to normal, Tyler removed his crushing weight from the sweet delicacy beneath him, and eased himself back to ground level. "Relax, baby," he murmured. "Let's get you out of these shackles."

Walking around the table, he untied her and removed the gag from her mouth. She was trembling, her green eyes large in her small face. "You good, Anna?" he murmured.

For several seconds, she said nothing.

Shit! Maybe he had pushed it with the ball gag. It was a hard limit even for one as experienced as he was.

Yet you gagged her. Why do you do that when you can't stomach being gagged yourself, huh? She loves you, and you just keep on punishing her for it, you sad fuck.

The accusation stuck in his throat, momentarily robbing him of his breath.

"I'm good," Anna whispered as she slipped shakily from table to floor. She stepped forward, and her left leg gave way. Scooping her up, he carried her into the shower room. Setting her down gently on the bench to the left of the now steaming showerhead. "Clean up, baby. I'll go see where we are. We should be near the cove by now."

"You're not staying with me?" She frowned.

"Do you want me to?"

"Yes. No. I—don't know."

"Then I'll leave you alone to figure it out. When you're ready, I'll be in the control room. 'The room where the controls are' to you." Tyler smirked, hoping to elicit at least one small laugh from her downturned lips, but Anna only nodded and closed her eyes.

Raking a hand through his hair, Tyler walked back to the control room, unease flowering in his stomach at the thought of losing the best thing that had ever happened to him, to his own selfish stupidity.

"Fuck."

He cared for the girl. *And yet you gagged her,* snarled his mind. *Way to fucking go, you dumb prick!*

This time, he didn't even try denying that little voice in his head. He was—he admitted to himself—one

182

stupid fucking asshole.

His phone buzzed, vibrating the console it sat on. Dr. Emily Reid's—the doctor he had taken Anna to when she had first arrived Wisconsin—name looped across the screen. He took the call on loudspeaker.

"Where the hell are you, Tyler?"

"Whatever happened to good old doctor-client civility?" he snapped.

"It disappeared after the first hour of trying to get hold of you and coming up empty. I repeat my question. Where are you?"

"I'm at the lake with Anna."

"You're at the lake with a sub?"

"What the fuck do you want, Em?"

Her exasperated sigh filled the cabin.

"I'm concerned about Anna's health."

"Why?"

"I'd rather speak with you both in person."

"You want to keep my business, and that surgery I rent to you, then you tell me now. I don't have time for your games today."

"You blackmailing me, Tyler?"

"Baby, seriously. You want to play this game with me?"

"You wouldn't dare."

"Try me. I'm sure your husband would just love to know how much you like being clamped, baby."

"You bastard."

"Your call, Doc."

"You tell anyone I broke patient protocol, and I will have your balls on a plate, Tyler Kane."

"Just fucking spill it, Em."

"The injection my colleague gave Anna wasn't what it was supposed to be. Tyler—Anna never got a depo."

"What the fuck do you mean she never got a depo. I was there. I saw it being administered."

"You saw an injection, but it wasn't a contraceptive injection. It was an antibiotic. My junior fucked up and misread my prescription notes."

"And I'm only just finding this out now why?"

"Because I only just discovered the mistake myself. Our contraceptive stock didn't tally correctly during our monthly checks. We were one up on our depo stock no matter which way we counted. Which means someone never got what she was supposed to get. I pulled every file that involved a contraceptive injection in the past month and cross-referenced every number against the patient's records. Anna's was the only one that didn't match up with the depo batch number. Her injection number matched Rocephin.

My junior fucked up, Tyler. Big style. So, if you have been having unprotected sex with the girl, then there's a damned good chance that she could be pregnant."

"Fuck!" He couldn't believe this.

"If you can make it to my office within the next hour, I can arrange for Anna to have a morning after."

"I'm out on the lake. There's no way we'll make it back in time. Can it wait until tomorrow?"

It was only a few weeks for fuck's sake. If there was anything there, another fucking day shouldn't make a difference, and if it did, there was always the abortion route.

"No, I don't think it can. I'll come on over to the house tonight."

"No good. We're staying at the marina tonight."

"Then I'll just have to come out there." She ended the call before he could argue.

Great. His last day with her and he had managed to scare the shit out of her and possibly impregnate her.

"Fuck it." He refused to let it dampen his mood. Em would come out to the lake, give her the damned pill, and boom! Problem sorted. He didn't know what all the fucking fuss was about. Abortions happened all the time. No biggie.

Easing up beside a mooring point, he cut the engine

and threw all the unpleasantries of the past hour to the back of his mind. The only thing that mattered to him right now was getting them safely ashore. Their feet would get wet, but for peace and tranquility on a shady, secluded shore, it was well worth it.

Killing the engine and dropping the ladders, he set off to find Anna. She was hanging upside down on the bed, blow drying her hair and fully dressed. A ring of blooming purple circled her right wrist. Marching over to his dresser, he picked up his diving watch and strapped it over the bruise. Anna watched, but said nothing.

"You ready?" he asked.

She switched off the hairdryer and sat up.

Grabbing the bristled brush from the coverlet, Tyler began to smooth out the tangled strands, enjoying the feeling of taking care of her in a manner other than sexual for once.

"Are you okay, baby?"

She nodded, her eyes refusing to meet his in the mirror.

"Have I done something to offend you, Anna?"

She shook her head, small pearly white teeth sinking into her bottom lip and gnawing hard. "I just need time to process—you know."

Sweeping up her hair, he secured it in his fist and looked for something to tie it with. She handed him a hair band, and he gently wound it around and let go, smoothing out her ponytail and feeling pleased with himself. He had never brushed a woman's hair before, but then he had never wanted to—until her. With a frown at the switch in his thoughts, he walked from the room before his mouth betrayed him and he said something he would regret.

ANNA

I can still feel the gag against my lips, the restraints chafing against my skin, rendering me helpless, a sexual toy without a fucking blow-up valve.

The whole experience has left me feeling dazed. Half of me feels used, dirty, sick to my stomach that anyone would want to do that type of shit to another person. And the other part, well, that was the confusing bit. I loved every delicious moment of it, the feel of the cloth grazing my skin, the power of Tyler as he took control, and the undiluted joy that had washed through me as he had fucked me with the momentum of a steam train.

That he was a steam train with problems was undeniable. One moment cold and commanding, angry with me for God knows what, and the next, gentle, caring, vulnerable. It was in those vulnerable moments that I loved him best.

Stifling a sob, I fall onto the bed, curl my knees into my chest, and weep for the pain I'm feeling, and the pain I know is still to come. I'm allowed this luxury, if only for a moment. And a moment is all I get as Tyler shouts down from above, his voice laced with irritation that I'm not already on deck.

Inhaling deeply, I wipe the tears from my eyes, pinch my cheeks, and, putting my best game face on, I roll from the bed and head up top.

Tyler is waiting for me on deck, hair still wet from his shower, chest bared, and dark eyes as unreadable as always. I force my best smile, and he extends his hand to me with a boyish smile all his own. The Tyler I love is back. I breathe a sigh of relief and slide my hand into his.

"I thought we could picnic here." He jumps down onto a deck that sways with the tide, his feet instantly becoming wet.

Seconds later, I'm standing with him, staring in open awe at the beauty of my surroundings. Paradise doesn't even begin to cover this place.

"Anna?"

"It's beautiful," I murmur.

"And all ours. You ready?"

"For what?"

"A dip." He smiles. "The jetty doesn't go all the way in. You're going to have to get wet, baby."

I am so not fucking ready, but he doesn't need any more of my emotional instability crap today, so I gulp down the fear threatening to undo me and force myself to nod. "You go first. I'll be right behind you. I just need to take my sandals and dress off."

He smiles radiantly and walks forward until there is nothing left to walk on. Sinking into the clear water, chest deep, basket high above his head, he wades toward the whitest, sandiest beach I have ever seen. Sand I so want to be sitting on, basking in the sun's warmth with Tyler Kane at my side. I can do this. I can. *Just fucking do it!* Breathing deep, I discard my dress, flip off my sandals, and face my fear of deep water head on.

My gaze locks on the man shaking moisture from his hair and setting out a picnic on the sands, and in less than a minute, I'm emerging victorious from the water like the strong girl Tyler Kane is molding me into. If nothing else, I'm glad I met Tyler Kane just for that attribute alone.

He watches me as I leave the water, dark eyes smoldering. I gaze back, safe in the knowledge that there are no gags at hand to silence me, and no shackles to bind and bruise. There is just us—one man, one woman and a whole lot of electricity charging the air between us with aged primal desire.

Without pausing to catch my breath and still dripping from my swim, I wrap my hands around his neck and kiss him with everything I feel for him but can never admit to.

I feel his confusion in the stiffness of his shoulders, and then he's with me, arms crushing me against him, his tongue devouring my own with a passion that has me moaning for more. God, I love him. Every delicious inch of him, and if only for this moment, he is mine.

I tug at the button to his shorts, desperate to feel him against me without the distraction of add-ons.

Tyler chuckles and disengages himself from my fervent fingers. "Much as I want to fuck you right now, Anna, I won't. So behave." He slaps my butt and kisses me chastely.

I moan in complaint.

"You could help me lay out the food if you're feeling restless." He points to the basket.

With a petulant pout, I slump down beside the basket and pass him wine, glasses, cheese, fruit, and a container filled with salad in one compartment and vegetable pasta in the next.

"You remembered?" I'm touched that he considered my dietary requirements.

"How could I forget after the simpering waiter event?"

"He wasn't simpering. He was merely attending to my needs."

"Baby, he wanted in your pants."

"Not everyone is as testosterone-fueled as you are, Tyler."

"Keep telling yourself that if it makes you feel better, Anna, but all men think like that. Most just don't have the balls to back it up. Or the stamina."

"As I recall, you had your own stamina problem a few minutes back."

Grabbing my hand, he shoves it against his straining erection. "I don't have problems getting a hard-on around you or fucking you regularly, Anna. But I do have issues fucking you while your mind is preoccupied elsewhere. Want to tell me what happened to you back there."

It's not a question.

I shake my head. "Not really. No."

"It might help if you talk about it."

"I tried that before, and you walked out. Remember?"

"I'm not walking now. Tell me. I want to know."

"You took my voice away!" I bark, and all the pain, all the helplessness I felt as a child colors my tone with venom.

"This isn't just about the gag, is it, Anna?"

"You took my voice away just like they did."

He falls to his knees, hands on my face, forcing me to look at him.

"What we did back there was consensual. If you didn't want it, all you had to do was say the safe-word, and I would have stopped."

"I couldn't. You put that thing in my mouth. I couldn't. I—"

Tears come unbidden to my eyes, thick and dense and choking as pain tears me up from the inside out.

He folds me within his arms, calming me with his gentle strength and warmth.

"You need to start trusting me, baby. I would never hurt you like they did."

"You already have."

He shuts his eyes and groans. "Fuck. You need to tell me how you're feeling, Anna, or this won't work."

"Ditto." My voice is strained with emotion.

"Fair point, Miss Wright. Okay. Was I pissed with

193

you back there? Yes."

"Why?"

"You need to understand, Anna, I have spent the past ten years in a world where women do as I say without question. And then you come along, with your smart little mouth, and you steal that control from me. Believe me, Anna, I'm more scared of you than you are of me." He swats my butt playfully. "You want to know a secret?" He lies back in the sand, pulling me with him.

I nod and inhale his sweetness, eyes closed, at one with the world for the first time in forever.

"I have never once had an erection outside of the dungeons. Then I saw you standing in that dingy little bar and—" He takes my hand and places it upon the pulsating bulge in his shorts. "This is what you do to me, Anna. You make me want to fuck for the sheer joy of being buried in you. Just you, baby! And feeling like that scares the shit out of me."

He encircles my back with his hands and rolls me beneath him, his erection prodding, needy, between my thighs.

"Let me make love to you, baby."

It's the first time he's said the word love in any context, and my heart soars as I lift my lips to his and kiss him with all the love I feel for him. If this is my last day with him, so be it. At least I'll have this moment to relive in the darker days ahead.

By the time we are sated, the sun is low in the sky, the wine warm, and my sex feels like it has just done ten rounds with Mike Tyson. Tyler lies snoring softly on my chest, his legs entwined with mine, sweat from our lovemaking slick between us. *Lovemaking.* I roll the word around on my tongue, savoring the beauty of it. And after today, it would all be gone. I would go home two million pounds richer, and Tyler Kane would step out of my life to move onto his next sexual adventure. The thought pierces my heart and leaves me gasping in pain. I roll out from beneath his sticky skin and, standing up, I wade forward into the sun-warmed water, tears streaming freely from my face.

"Anna?"

Wiping my eyes quickly, I glance back. Tyler, waking up, looks every inch the charming man I know he is, and not the cold, heartless bastard he pretends to be.

"I needed to pee," I lie.

Tyler shoves his feet back into his shorts and stands up hurriedly, glancing at his watch. "Fuck! We're supposed to be back at the dock. Bert will be waiting to take Silver."

"We better get back then." I smile, and without preamble, start swimming back toward the boat, all fear of water erased in my eagerness to hide my pain from him.

Five minutes later, and I'm fully dressed in a red backless shift dress, red lacy underwear and silk nude stockings. And all thanks to Mara. My liking of Tyler's ex-sub slides up a notch.

"You could have waited for me." He drops the picnic basket and shakes his dark hair free of droplets.

"I like your hair all wet like that." I smile, inserting small diamond studs into my ears.

"Flattery will get you everywhere, Miss Wright." He grins.

"I do hope so, Mr. Kane. Your suit is in the bathroom. Go get changed before I jump your bones."

He laughs loudly and nibbles my neck before disappearing into the bathroom. I am so not going to last another day feeling like this. And if I do it, I know I'll only suffer for it later. Another tear streaks across my cheek, and I wipe it impatiently away. He must never learn how much I care for him. Never. But how can I hide it when these damn tears refuse to stop?

"Anna!" I turn too quickly, and his brows drop, necktie hanging limply from his hands. "You crying, baby?"

Fuck, his concern is making me feel worse.

I shake my head and turn back to the task at hand, applying my mascara without looking like a damned panda in the process. "I'm fine, just poked my eye with the mascara brush."

He turns the chair, and then I'm facing him, green eyes on brown.

"Then why are two eyes streaming and not just one? Want to tell me what's really going on, baby? You have done nothing but cry since you woke up this morning."

"It's nothing. Honestly, I'm fine."

"Is it still that damned gag?"

I kiss him softly and stand up. "Go get ready. It's nothing. Honestly."

Strong hands grip my shoulders. "Anna. Tell me."

"I—I don't want to go home tomorrow." There, I've said it.

Relief floods his face, and Tyler Kane smiles. "Then don't."

"But I have college to get back to. I have—"

"A man who doesn't want you to go sitting right in

front of you."

My heart races giddily within my chest. Tyler doesn't want me to go?

"Why?"

"Apart from the mind-blowing sex, you mean?"

"But I can't give you what you really want. I'm not a submissive, Tyler."

"And I don't want you to be. I like that smart mouth of yours calling me out, baby. I like waking up with you in my bed, knowing that I'm the only one who has ever touched you, fucked you. The thought of you going home and someone else bringing you to orgasm, baby, it's been driving me insane. Stay with me, Anna. I'll do whatever it takes to make you happy."

"Full monogamy?"

"Baby, you had that from the first fucking moment I laid eyes on you." He grins. "Now dry your tears. We'll be docking in a few minutes, and I don't want Bert thinking I'm a bigger bastard than he already thinks I am." Kissing my nose, Tyler stands up and whistles his way back onto the deck.

Voices drift through to me, and I wipe my tears away, curious to know who the other voice belongs to as I join Tyler on deck. He's shouting something to an older man who looks like he just stepped from the cover of an "Angler's Friends" advert, white beard, pipe, and all. I smile down, and he doffs his cap respectfully before turning his attention back to Tyler and barking instructions at him.

I watch the interaction in fascination. Tyler Kane taking orders and looking like a chastised schoolboy. The image softens my heart even further.

"You're a damned novice, boy. Look at her side! I'm gonna have to get that sanded and repainted. How many times have I told you to stay out of Sandy Cove? But you just don't fuckin' listen, do you? Just like your daddy before you. Stubborn and foolhardy is what you are."

Tyler's face is suffused with heat as he coils in the excess rope and ties it off, his teeth gritted with the effort of his labors.

Bert grabs the ropes and ties off from the other end before standing back and waiting for us to join him.

Tyler snorts something uncomplimentary and slides out the gangplank before grabbing my hand and helping me back down to dry land.

"Here, you cantankerous little gnome. Take her, and do what needs doing. And just for the record, I didn't put that scratch there. It must have been Mara."

"Yeah, and my Granny is fuckin' Shakira. Miss." He

doffs his cap again and is on board before I can muster a reply.

"Wow!"

"Yeah, you got that right, baby! If it weren't for the fact that he knows more about boats than anyone I have ever met, I would have sacked his poisonous little dwarf ass years ago. Hairy little bastard." He scowls after the Silver. Then his eyes flick back to me, and he grins. "C'mon!" Lacing his fingers through my own again, he walks me up a concrete drive toward a large timber house.

"This was my father's bolt hole from reality. Frank and I, we come here fishing whenever we get the chance.

"You said 'was'. Doesn't your father use it anymore?" The thought of this beautiful house lying empty week after week makes me feel like crying. A house like this deserves a family.

"My parents died when I was just a boy, Anna. Mrs. Greene was appointed my legal guardian until I was of legal age to manage my own affairs." He opens the front door and waits for me to precede him, then steps inside himself. "Welcome to my family condo, Anna. Dinner awaits. I hope!" He snorts.

Inside, a table for two has been set in a large open

plan beamed space, and next to that, a bain-marie with an assortment of plates all carefully wrapped in tin foil.

Two bottles of champagne sit in a bucket swimming with semi-melted ice. Seems we're late after all.

Pulling a chair out, he seats me with undivided attention and proceeds to plate up. "Brie ravioli. Help yourself to the salad." He pours a glass of champagne, plates his own meal and seats himself across from me.

"You treat all your women like this, Mr. Kane?" I slide one of the delicate looking parcels into my mouth.

"I've never had a woman before, Anna. Not in a relationship sense anyway." He sips at the champagne and concentrates on his food.

Go figure. Tyler Kane is nervous. I smile and spear another ravioli.

"What about your subs?"

"You really want to know?" he asks, eyes glittering over the candles.

I nod and chew.

"They were trained professionals, willing to serve my most carnal needs. Rina vetted them, my lawyers drew up the contracts, and I supported them financially until their contracts ended."

"How long did the contracts last?"

"Six months. And never the same sub twice."

"Weren't you afraid of STDs?"

"Anna, I never fuck without screening, and even then, I use protection."

"You haven't with me."

He pours another glass and downs it in one. Why is he so nervous?

"No. I haven't." He scowls and looks at his plate.

"Why?"

"Because nothing is premeditated with you, Anna. From total control to nothing. I don't understand it myself, baby, and believe me, I have racked my brain trying to. I can't leave you alone. You're like a fucking virus that no matter how much I want to rid myself of it, I can't. I go to sleep, I fucking dream of you. I go to work, I can think of *nothing* but you. You want to know why I brought you here today?"

I nod, too afraid to breathe, to blink.

"Because I thought that once you saw me as I really am, the way I am with you right now, you might be persuaded to stay with me. What you said back there, about not wanting to go—I feel the same way. And, baby, it scares the hell out of me." He drops his fork and pushes his plate away.

202

I sip at my champagne, the cogs in my brain whirring as I try to compute just what he's saying. Tyler Kane, property magnate, and sexual God wants me—little Anna Wright from Glasgow—to stay with him. But for how long? Six months just like the others? And when he gets bored, what then? I go back home and try to stick back together the pieces of the heart he's shattered. I shake my head, tears pricking my eyes. No matter how much I want to stay, I'm just not that brave.

"For fuck's sake, Anna. You want me to get down on my knee and produce a fucking ring? 'Cause, baby, if that's what it takes…"

I snort through a mouthful of wine and grab a napkin to mop up the fallout. He's even more naive than I am. No one falls in love and lives happily ever after, not after four weeks of kinky sex and not much else. I stop coughing. "Fuck. You're serious."

He stands up and begins to pace, thrusting his hands through his hair in naked agitation.

"That's the stupidest thing I have ever heard. You don't know me, Tyler. You know *nothing* about me."

"You think I haven't gone over that in my head a million times? You think I like being at your fucking mercy? I don't have a choice here, Anna, I wish to hell

I did!"

I blink and snap my mouth shut. What can I say? Nada, that's what.

"The first time I set eyes on you in that bar—" He shakes his head, linking his fingers behind his neck and exhaling loudly.

I frown in total disbelief that this gorgeous man could care for me. He is so beautiful, and I am just so—well, just so.

"Something inside of me flipped, and it hasn't flipped back, baby. So please, do me a favor and just think about it."

"What? Think about what, Tyler? Marrying you? Staying with you? Being your—what? Your new sub? 'Cause if that's what you want, Tyler, you got the wrong girl. I can't…live like that. I'm sorry."

He moans and, dropping to his knees before me, rests his forehead against mine. "I have thought many things about you over the last few weeks, baby, but a sub was never one of them. And living without you isn't open to negotiation."

I don't believe this. Any second, I'm going to wake up and realize it's just a dream.

"Fuck's sake, Anna. I'm down on my knees here. Say something!"

I snort in disbelief that I'm actually considering telling him just how much I care.

"Anna. Please." He grips my face, dark eyes scorching into my own.

I bite my lip in deliberation. Fuck it! I meet his gaze head on and confess what I never thought I would have the nerve to. "I'm in love with you, Tyler Kane. But if you don't feel the same way, it's a waste of my time—"

He kisses me in a way that he never has before. It's a kiss that lays him open to me, bare bones and all, and I realize in that tender moment that Tyler Kane is just as scared as I am, maybe even more so.

A knock at the door and my fairy tale moment ends as abruptly as it started.

Tyler scowls. "Fuck! I forgot she was coming."
"Who?"

"My doctor. She phoned me this afternoon. Seems they fucked up your contraceptive injections and forgot to tell us."

"But we've been—" Oh, my sweet Lord, the number of times he's fucked me without protection! I groan and flop away from him, head on the table, hands over my head.

In the background of my misery, I can hear Tyler

greeting the good doctor, and lifting my head up wearily, I force a smile on my face.

"Hello, Doctor."

She looks past Tyler and smiles, and I wonder if she has ever fucked him. Seems everyone else around him has, so why not her as well? God, I need to stop this. He had a fucking life before me. I need to get over it. She walks forward and shakes my hand with a look of concern that only doctors seem able to carry off with any real emotion.

"Em, please, and I am so, so sorry about all of this, Anna. Can we go somewhere more private?"

"Here's fine." His tone is saying it's not up for discussion.

She ignores him, but I'm not that brave.

"Here's fine," I reiterate.

"Okay, here it is. Tyler has informed me that since he thought you were covered against an unwanted pregnancy, he hasn't been using precautions like he should have been." The good Dr. Em flicks Tyler a disapproving look, and he glares right back.

"This is your fuck up, Em. Not mine."

"Regardless. You should have—"

"Can we just stop with the blame game please and get this over with."

Two sets of angry eyes look in my direction and mellow instantly.

"I want to give you a morning after pill, Anna. But before I do, I need to ask some questions and test your urine. Is that okay?"

"Can't you just give her the damned pill?"

She ignores him with a grunt of annoyance and places a thermometer into my ear. A minute later it beeps, and she removes it, glances at the result and places it back in her pocket.

"Your periods are regular, a twenty-eight-day cycle, yes?"

Fuck! Where is she going with this? "Yes," I murmur.

"And your last cycle ended when?"

I do the math in my head. Shit. "Thirty days ago."

"So, you're late by two days. Yes?"

I nod.

"And have you ever been late before, Anna?"

"A few days maybe, nothing more."

"And you have engaged in intercourse today?"

Heat suffuses my cheeks, and I gaze down at my nails. "Yes."

"How many times, Anna?"

"Is this fucking necessary?"

"In order for me to ascertain risk versus benefits? Yes. It is. Anna?" she asks again.

"Um, five times.

"And during those—"

"Five times, Doc. I ejaculated into Anna five fucking times! Okay?"

"And before today?"

"A lot. That's all you need to know," Tyler snarls.

"Feel free to leave anytime you want, Tyler."

"And leave Anna in your incapable hands? Not a chance in hell!"

She snaps her attention back to me and holds up a small stick-like instrument in front of my face. "Anna, this device checks your luteinizing hormone levels. If they are higher than normal, giving you an emergency contraceptive pill would be a waste of your time and mine."

"What do you want me to do?" I ask, stunned that I might be pregnant by this beautiful yet fucked-up man. A man who has spanked me, buggered me, tied me up, and performed all other kinds of kinky shit on me. A man I have known less than a month and would never have slept with at all if he hadn't bought my virginity in an online auction.

Fuck! What type of romance tale is that to tell your

kids?

How did you meet Mummy, Daddy?

She auctioned off her virginity, son, and I bought it.

I drag my hands across my eyes in all out exhaustion. Why is nothing ever simple with Tyler Kane?

"You need to pee on the end here and bring it back to me, okay?"

"That's it?" I take the stick-like object and follow Tyler toward the bathroom.

Five minutes later, and I'm waiting numbly for the results.

The good doc shakes her head and sits down. "Your basal temp registered at point five above typical, Anna. And your menstruation dates suggest that you were at your most fertile two weeks ago. Your luteinizing hormone is registering as high, and you're late. Add to that the number of times Tyler has ejaculated into you, and I would say that there's a pretty good chance you're pregnant. Giving you an emergency contraceptive would be a waste of time."

She pats my knee consolingly and stands up. "I suggest you perform a pregnancy test. If it's positive—which I'm sure it will be—come into my surgery and we'll talk about the options available to you. And since we're being candid, Anna, I think it would be a miracle if it came back negative. Tyler." She nods and lets herself out. The door clicks shut in her wake.

From fairy tale to nightmare and all in less than five seconds.

Tyler has left off the shoulder stroking and is pacing furiously. Not that I care what he does right now. I'm too numb to care.

"I'll set up a termination date. The sooner we get this over with the better."

"I want to go home." Not home Wisconsin but home Scotland, as far away as I can from Tyler Kane and his murderous plans.

He stops pacing and spins me around to face him.

"I want to go home," I repeat.

"We can fix this, Anna. Trust me. Okay? Another couple of weeks and it will just be a bad memory."

"Can we go, please?"

"No. I arranged to spend the night here, and I'm not going to let this shit change my fucking plans. Come."

He grips my hand firmly, and I yank it back.

"Seriously, I might be pregnant, and you want to fuck? No." I shake my head venomously. *What is wrong with this man?*

"Where you're concerned, Anna, it's all I want to do. Every second of every fucking day since I met you.

And I'm really sorry if you find that offensive, but that's just the way it is. As for the other thing, if you are pregnant, you won't be for long. End of discussion."

Standing up, I walk toward a door that only a short time ago, I had entered through with such joy in my heart.

"I'm sorry, Tyler. I just can't be near you anymore."

"Don't you dare, Anna. Don't you fucking dare walk out on me."

"I'm sorry, Tyler." I pick the small clutch bag I brought from the boat with me, and close the door on the only real emotion I have ever felt. Yet I can't bring myself to regret it. Not for one second.

I walk down the pathway, expecting Tyler to run out of the house and pull me back in, but the door remains resolutely closed. Pulling out my phone I call for a taxi, giving Silver Bay marina as the address. A taxi glides into the marina ten minutes later and I climb inside, my face dry, my heart shriveled. I tell myself I got what I came for. And I'm still repeating that same lie to myself the following day as I fly over the Atlantic on my way back to Scotland.

ANNA

I trace the rain river with my fingertips. Following the small glistening baubles of moisture, until they merge with shiny gloss plastic designed to keep the elements out, and the heat in. So the estate agent had spun me before I had bought the old cottage in the middle of nowhere, and everywhere.

Nowhere was a country estate consisting of one renovated gatekeeper's cottage and a whole load of sparrow-infested hedgerows. Everywhere was a twenty-minute drive to Glasgow's city center and all the social diversity that brought with it.

Not that I cared about society, diverse or otherwise. I was too busy trying to piece my heart back together after the tornado that had been Tyler Kane fragmented it.

"You'll have to talk to him sooner or later, you know?" Steph looks at me as she would a wounded puppy. Do I really look that pitiful? I push the thought aside and concentrate on forming the words that will alleviate her worry.

"I will, just not yet, okay?"

"Anna, I'm worried about you."

I need to divert the subject onto safer ground.

"How's Frank?"

"Nipping at me to talk sense into you."

"Tell him I'll talk to his brother soon, okay?"

"Jesus, Anna. You can't even say his name."

"Please, Steph…don't. I can't deal with you being angry with me right now."

Wiping wet fingers on my sweater, I stand up and meander my way toward a kitchen that Tyler's money helped build.

"I'm not—Jesus, Anna I'm not mad at you. I'm mad at myself for setting you up with Tyler fucking Kane in the first place. The guy's a dick with a capital D."

I shake my head and grab a mug from the cupboard. "He's not a dick, Steph."

"My arse he isn't. You've been back here two months now, and you look worse every time I see you."

"Gee, thanks."

"You know what I mean. If it weren't for Tyler, you wouldn't be in this fucking mess."

"And by 'mess' you mean pregnant?"

213

"No, by 'mess', I mean an emotional fucking wreck. It's not good for you or the baby, Anna."

She has a point there. Between the morning sickness and thoughts of Tyler Kane ruining my sleep, I feel like a washed-out dishrag.

I hold my hand out placatingly. "Okay. Point taken."

"And I'd worry less if you moved back to Glasgow. Whatever possessed you to buy a house in the middle of nowhere with a baby on the way? What if you fell? Or went into labor early."

"Tea?" I ask, amused by her hostile concern.

"You sit, I'll pour," she commands.

I do as I am told, grateful that I have a friend like her to keep me sane in this mess I've created for myself.

"So—" She hands me a mug and sits down across from me, tucking her legs beneath her in full-on relax mode. "When are you coming back to classes?"

"I'm booked in for next semester. Maggie said she would help with the babysitting as long as I don't expect her to stay overnight."

"I haven't seen Mags since you left for—well, you know. How is she?"

"Really good actually. Since I bought her the flat, she's registered with the Open University. She starts a degree in social care as soon as the paper packages arrive."

"Good for her. You tell her about Tyler yet?"

"Is he still breathing?"

"That's a no then."

I sip my tea and nod. "Yep. That's a no."

We slip into easy silence. Ten minutes in and Steph's phone vibrates to life.

"You know who that will be, don't you?"

"Switch it off then."

"Sacrilege." Steph without social media at hand is like jam without toast. Never gonna happen. I chuckle and sip.

She slaps the phone out onto her lap on full speakerphone.

"You lied to me, Steph. She's not in class. She hasn't even registered for a class this year. So, I'm going to ask you one last time, and you had better tell me the fucking truth. Where is she?"

"Depends."

"On what?" God I've missed hearing his voice.

Hiding my face in my mug, I count silently to ten in a vain attempt to slow my traitorous heart.

"On where you are."

"Tell me where she is, Steph.".

"What makes you think I even know where she is, Tyler?"

"I'm done playing this game." The line goes dead.

"I have to put up with that four, five times a day. Is he always so fucking domineering?"

I nod my head. "Pretty much."

"Geez, Anna. No wonder you left."

I place down the mug and shake my head.

"I didn't leave because of his temper, Steph. I left because I wanted to keep this baby."

"And he didn't? Because that's not what he's telling Frank. Anna, he told Frank he wants you and the baby in his life. And trust me, from what I've experienced of Tyler Kane over the past few weeks, he has no intention of going back to Wisconsin without you. He is one determined son of a bitch."

I stand up and lift the empty mug. "I have my first scan this afternoon. You want to come?"

"Can't." She stands up and pockets her phone. "Franks meeting me for lunch at Nandos. You can meet us there afterwards if you want."

"And risk Frank's niggling? No thanks." I kiss her proffered cheek and just like that, I'm left all alone to deal with the emotional fall out of Tyler Kane all over again. I need a distraction—maybe a walk in the rain?

Grabbing my wellies and faded old parka coat, I shove them on, and step out into rain that falls straight and hard with not a puff of wind in sight.

I roll up my hood, pulling the drawstrings in tight as I begin walking slowly up the old pot-holed road with no destination in mind. Not that there's anywhere to go unless you like rolling fields and a gray skyline obscured by drizzle.

Still, it's peaceful, and right now, peaceful is what I need.

A rumble in the distance announces a thunderstorm, so I turn back, not willing to risk a tree falling on my head or worse, a direct hit. Three weeks ago, I had watched a farmer tow a dead cow from a large puddle in the middle of the field opposite my bedroom window. Seems the cow had been standing in the water minding its own business when forked lightning had hit and fried its brains. Now, when I'm outside and I hear thunder, I get quick smart indoors.

But it's not thunder I hear now. Thunder doesn't roll up behind you and spit gravel against your calves.

I turn and wish to hell I hadn't. Tyler Kane is jumping out of his four by four and marching through the rain toward me, his beautiful face dark with rage.

I sprint toward the cottage—not an easy thing to do when you're wearing thick rubber wellies—and bolt myself inside.

Several seconds later and Tyler's hand makes hard contact with the wood of my front door. "I can stand here all fucking day, Anna! All night too if that's what it takes."

"How the hell did you get this address, Tyler?" If it was Steph, I am so going to kill her.

"I tracked your friend's phone. Now, are you going to let me in or do I have to break down this damn door? 'Cause, baby, you know I will."

"I'm pretty sure that's illegal, you know."

"Nothing's illegal if you have the money. Now open up this damn door, or so help me—"

"Go away, Tyler. The contract's up. I don't have to do what you say anymore."

"Open the door, Anna." His voice is quiet, and all the more dangerous for it.

"No."

I hold my breath expecting another bang, but there is nothing except the sound of my own heart hammering loudly within my ears.

"You need to learn to lock your doors, Anna."

I spin around, and there he is, all glowering dark

eyes and sexy dark hair.

"I didn't think I needed to." I gasp, trying desperately to breathe over the fire in my chest. But no matter how hard I drag at the air, my lungs refuse to co-operate. Blackness tinges my vision. My heart stutters, dies, and my legs give out.

TYLER

A heady cocktail of emotions surged through his body when he looked at Anna Wright. Hatred, anger, love, lust, adoration, fear—it was all there, and it all transgressed quickly to horror the second she collapsed before him.

He surged forward, catching Anna mid-fall and cradling her against his chest. "I got you, baby. It's okay. It's okay, Anna."

She groaned and fluttered open those beautiful green eyes of hers.

Tyler smiled reassuringly and, scooping her up, he carried her toward a quaint little settee set in front of an open fire.

Anna tried to slap him away, but he was in no mood. "Anna, stop it. I'm not going to fucking hurt you. Jesus, I just need to know you didn't hurt yourself."

"I'm fine. Get your hands off me, Tyler." She sat up and pushed him back. "I don't want you here. Please, just go back to Wisconsin and leave me alone."

He stood up and marched into the kitchen, looking for a kettle and coffee and finding it quickly in the small space. *Who the hell had designed this cottage, a fucking hobbit?*

"Tyler, I'm serious. Please, just leave us alone."

"Us?"

"Us. As in me and my baby, Tyler. The same baby you wanted me to abort. Remember?"

Shame at the way he had treated her in the condo washed anew through his veins. "I should never have said those things to you. I'm a total dick for even thinking them in the first place. Anna, I'm sorry."

"Don't you dare try that on me, Tyler Kane. Don't you fucking dare. You decided I would be having an abortion without even consulting me on what I want-ed."

He threw coffee granules into the empty mug. "I'm asking you now, Anna."

She blinked at him before lowering her gaze.

"It's too late, Tyler. We made this beautiful little life, and you wanted to destroy it because it didn't fit in with your fucking daily schedule."

"Is that why you left?"

"Part of the reason, yes."

At last! Now he was getting somewhere. Picking up the kettle, he sloshed water into his mug, stirred and pulled down another cup from the shelf. "Can I make you a tea? Coffee?"

She shook her head. He lifted his mug and sat across from her huddled little body, desperate to touch her just to make sure she was real, but afraid that if he did, she would disappear and leave him all alone again.

So he sat forward, mug cradled within his hands to stop himself from reaching for her. "And the other part?" he asked.

She sighed heavily, uncurled her long legs, and walked towards a door he assumed led to the bedroom.

Tyler stood up and followed, not wanting to lose sight of her again. Never again. He leaned against the bedroom door, sipping the deplorable coffee to hide his nervousness at being so close to her again.

"Anna, what was the other part?"

Sitting on the edge of what he assumed was her bed, Anna began peeling her boots, sodden socks, and clinging jeans from her legs. That done, she picked up a pair of black chinos beside her on the bed and stuffed her feet inside, zipping up the side and tying her hair back with a band from her bedside table. She looked tired and deflated, but she was just as beautiful as the first day he had seen her. Even more so now that she carried their baby within her. A life he had wanted nothing to do with until she walked out of his life and took that small life with her.

"I didn't want the lifestyle you offered, Tyler. This little cottage, the rain, cooking cupcakes, painting—this is what I want, Tyler, and you just don't fit in here no matter how much I might want you to." She stuffed her feet into black leather flats and grabbed a set of keys and her purse from a chaise lounge nestled at the bottom of the bed.

A small sliver of silver glistened at the edge of her waistband, and he stopped breathing. She was still wearing his chain. The knowledge stirred his heart to new heights. Anna Wright still cared for him no matter what she said to the contrary.

"I don't mean to be rude, but I have a pre-na—" She bit her lip and tried to cover. "I have an appointment."

"And, as the father, I have every right to be there with you."

She shouldered past him, but she wasn't getting off that lightly.

"Anna, whatever issues we have, you have no right

to shut me out of this. It's my baby as much as it is yours no matter what you think of me."

"I don't think anything of you, Tyler. Not anymore."

"Then me being there shouldn't be a problem. Stay here." He brushed past her and opened the front door. "I'll get the car. I don't want you driving in this. It's not safe."

"My safety is no longer your concern, Tyler."

"As long as you're carrying my child, it's the only thing that matters, Anna." Without waiting for her reply, he leaped out into the downpour and sprinted towards his car, grateful that he had driven all the way up the pot-holed track and not abandoned his Land Rover at the bottom, as he had originally planned to do. Not that it mattered. He was already soaked through to his skin.

Several minutes later, and the young woman he had spent the past three months losing sleep over was sitting silently at his side.

"Where's the appointment?"

"Regent Gardens Medical Centre, Kirkintilloch."

He punched the name into his satnav and slowly eased them through the potholes until gravel gave way to good old tarmac.

"That's one hell of a road for a pregnant lady to

drive over every day."

"I don't drive it every day."

"So, what? You just nest up in your little mouse hole back there and have everything delivered?"

"It's not a mouse hole."

"Baby, it's a mouse hole. Fuck!"

He slammed on the brakes as what looked like a hare bounded out in front of them. The action jarred Anna forward. "Shit. Anna, are you okay?"

"Please, tell me we didn't hit it." Her green eyes were wide and pleading in a face too pale to be healthy.

He shook his head. "No. More's the pity. You sure you're okay?"

She nodded and glanced off into the field. Probably looking for the damn thing just to make sure he wasn't lying.

"Anna, it's fine. I saw its furry little rump disappear into the ditch."

She nodded but kept her gaze fixed on the fields passing them.

Twenty-five minutes later, and Tyler was driving down the shabbiest little town center he had ever set eyes on. To say it was in need of an overhaul would have been an understatement.

"Park in Tesco's car park," Anna directed.

"In here?" The car bounced over yet another damn rut. "What the hell is it with this place, potholes and never-ending bloody rain? It's a mystery to me why anyone wants to stay here."

"You're free to go back home anytime you want," she challenged, her eyes closing in a face paler than any he had ever seen.

"Anna, what's wrong?"

She pursed her lips and dipped her head down between her legs, her breathing shallow and fast.

Tyler rubbed her back, feeling as useless as he probably was.

Anna slapped him away. "I'm fine. It's just morning sickness."

"Is there anything I can do?" Damn, he felt so fucking inept.

"Go back home and leave me the hell alone."

He shook his head and chuckled. "Nice try, Anna. I'll go see if I can rustle up a sick bowl. Stay here."

She mumbled something between clenched lips that didn't sound so sweet. Tyler smiled and strode with purpose toward a square-shaped building bearing the name Regent Gardens Medical Centre.

Double doors swished open, and Tyler walked toward a small desk manned with one solitary frigging receptionist.

Ignoring a sign asking him to wait, he approached the receptionist. Miss Goofy Receptionist blinked, her face suffusing with undiluted heat.

"I need a sick bowl for my wife." There. That should dull her fucking interest. I'm married, honey. Back off. *Liar,* his mind hissed accusingly. *Not if I get my way,* he threw back just as heatedly.

"Your wife?"

"My wife," he repeated with bite.

She dipped down, all fingers and thumbs as she lifted a hat from the pyramid of gray at her feet. Before she could hand it to him, he snatched it from her and was running back to Anna.

She was panting, head between her knees, face paler than he had ever seen it.

"Than—thanks," she mumbled between desperate gasps.

Sliding an arm around her waist, Tyler helped her out of the four by four, and amazingly, she didn't slap him off. Hope flickered brightly within him as she gave her name to the same starry-eyed receptionist from earlier.

"Anna Wright. I have an ante-natal appointment."

227

She was immediately directed down a corridor to the left. "Thank you." She smiled weakly at the receptionist, and allowed him to pull her in just that little bit closer.

"How you feeling now?" he whispered against her hair. God, she smelled good. He had forgotten just how good until now.

"Better, now that I'm out of that damn oven you call a car." She sat herself down in a small empty waiting area with no water or staff at hand. He made a mental note to arrange private care as soon as he got back to his office. This was not how he wanted Anna or his son to be cared for prenatally.

His son! The thought slapped him hard enough to leave an imprint. Up until this moment, his top priority had been to find her, and now that he had, his thoughts shifted to the undeniable fact that she carried his child within her small body. A body he had whipped and suspended from the fucking ceiling with chains. Jesus! What if that was his daughter hanging from those chains? He would rip the guy apart who did that to her. Anna had been right in what she'd said back in Wisconsin—he *was* fucked up.

"Anna?"

A uniformed nurse smiled warmly at them and

handed Anna a cup of water. "I'm Bernadette. How you feeling, honey?"

"Like somebody put me through a wringer and came back for a second go."

"Morning sickness?"

Anna nodded and gulped down the water before handing the plastic cup back.

"Try hard boiled sweets. Worked a wee treat when I was pregnant. How's dad holding up?"

"Dad's still in shock," he answered honestly.

"My husband is still in shock and our son is four years old now." She laughed and taking Anna from him, the nurse fished a candy from her pocket. "Suck this, Anna. It'll help."

Anna smiled her thanks as he walked on behind, slightly disgruntled that he wasn't the one with his hand around her waist.

"In here, honey."

The room was dark with a small computer screen in one corner and a white papered clinical bed in the other.

"If you could pop yourself up onto the bed, Anna, lie back for me and shift your waistband down a little. Good girl. Mr.—?" She looked at him with an apologetic smile.

"Tyler. My name, it's Tyler."

"Well, Tyler, if you stand just the other side of Anna. You ready?"

He nodded in time with Anna. Fuck! When had he ever felt this nervous?

"Sorry, Anna. This gel might be cold."

Anna winced as the clear gel was squirted across her skin and kept her eyes fixed firmly on the screen.

The friendly nurse placed a small scanner type object on Anna's belly, and the static on the screen gave way to a small body with a flickering little dot of white at its center.

"Is that her heart?" Anna gasped.

"Sure is. And by the looks of things—" A few small lines appeared as the nurse took measurements. "I would say you're about ten weeks pregnant, Anna. Is that what you thought?"

"I didn't know for sure, but that ties in with the dates. Is everything else okay?"

"Everything else seems fine and the morning sickness, although horrible, is a good sign. Tyler, you're awful quiet there. You okay?"

Tears stung his eyes, and there was a lump stuck in his throat. But other than that, he had never felt better.

"I'm good." He couldn't tear his eyes from the small beating heart of his son, or daughter—he was hoping for the former. A heart he had helped make. His own heart swelled with love and tipped him over the edge of keeping it together to total blubbering mess.

"Excuse me." He rushed outside of the room and laid his head against the corridor's wall. That was his child, that small helpless little being growing inside of her. And he had wanted to tear it to pieces bit by fucking bit. No wonder she had wanted nothing to do with him. He raked his hands through his hair in full on self-disgust.

"Tyler?" Anna stood in the doorway looking shell-shocked.

"I'll see you in four weeks, Anna."

Anna nodded into the dark room behind her and closed the door softly. "Here." She extended a small picture toward him, and he took it with shaking fingers.

He gazed incredulously at the small black and white image as tears again pricked at his eyes.

Without a word, she hugged him to her, and he gripped on for dear life as the emotions he had spent a lifetime building a wall around burst free.

"C'mon." She took his hand in hers and tugged him

out into daylight again.

"Anna—"

"Can we do this back at the cottage? Please."

He nodded and opened the passenger door for her.

Twenty-five minutes and a whole lot of chassis rocking and tire bumping later, and Anna was making tea. "You okay, Tyler?"

He took the mug from her cold little hands and shook his head.

"Want to talk about it?" She sat down next to him.

"I am so sorry, Anna. I am so…"

Tears slipped from his eyes yet again, and this time, he didn't try to wipe them away.

"What happened back there, Tyler?"

"I fell in love," he whispered, swiping uselessly at a tear. "I looked at that little thumping heart and felt like I was finally…home."

Anna folded her arms around his shoulders, and he sank his head to her chest, listening to the calming thrum of her fragile heart.

"You get why I left now?"

He nodded, not trusting himself to speak.

"It's tough, isn't it, knowing you're responsible for the safety of something so small."

He laid a hand on her belly, and her heart quickened

beneath his ear.

"I want us to be a family, Anna. I want this baby born back home in Wisconsin in the same bed I was born in. I want my ring on your finger and last but by no means least, baby, I want my name at the end of yours. I won't ever hurt you again, Anna. The play room, the dungeons, they're gone. Please. I just want you to come back home with me, Anna."

"You got rid of your toys?" She smirked.

He nodded. "The bigger ones. Yes."

"And you want me to marry you?"

"The sooner, the better."

She smiled, stroked his face, and he forgot to breathe all over again.

"I missed you, Tyler Kane." Her words stirred new hope within him, and lifting his wet face to hers, he kissed her with all the love he had within him and then some. She moaned into his mouth, and it took all of his restraint to slide his lips free of hers.

"Baby, I swore on my way here today that I was going to do things properly with you this time."

"And by properly you mean what exactly?" She smiled and traced her fingers across his straining zip.

"Jesus, Anna, you're not making this easy for me are you?"

233

She pulled her hand back. "You're serious?"

He had never been more serious about anything in his entire life, and if he was completely honest with himself, it was more fun than getting straight down to business. "I had it all planned out in my head. I was going to ask you to dinner, and then maybe a movie."

"And now?"

He sat a little taller and coughed nervously. "I know it's a bit late but—will you go out to dinner with me, Anna. No sex, no foreplay, just me taking you out on a date. What do you say?"

Anna's eyes glimmered with moisture. "I would be honored to go on a date with you, Tyler Kane."

Happiness exploded within him. For a man who had spent his life fucking without the preamble of dating, he was relishing every moment of asking her out.

He stood up, and leaning down briefly, he kissed her wet cheek.

"I'll pick you up tonight at six then?"

She shook her head. "I arranged to meet with Mags tonight. The street woman I told you about?"

Mags? Ahhh! Mags. She must be the woman who had pushed her into a college education and protected her during her times on the street. He wanted to meet the great lady himself, but not tonight. Tonight, he needed to prove to himself that he could give her the space she needed to breathe.

"Tomorrow then? Say six? I'll pick you up here."

"Are you leaving?"

Fuck. She actually, sounded disappointed!

"I don't want to outstay my welcome." He smiled, kissed her cheek again, and walked towards the door.

"Tyler, stay. Please."

His sac tightened in anticipation of emptying its contents deep within her, but he ignored it. "Tomorrow, little one. Six o'clock." He closed the door, grinning like a damned schoolboy as he walked back to the Land Rover. And for the first time in his life, Tyler Kane couldn't wait for tomorrow to come.

Thank you for purchasing and reading, Lost In Kane.

Book two in the Master Series, Loving Kane, will be with you shortly. In the meantime, please feel free to visit Amanda at www.asmythauthor.com, and pick up your free copy of Master Kane, scene one; Tyler's first scene as a Master.

Enjoy,

Amanda xx

Lightning Source UK Ltd.
Milton Keynes UK
UKOW04f0626210717
305775UK00001B/79/P